Look out for more escapades

MASTER CROOK'S CRIME ACADEMY

BURGLARY FOR BEGINNERS

ROBBERY FOR RASCALS

MASTER CROOK'S
CRIME ACADEMY

CLASSES IN KIDNAPPING

SS

MASTER CROOK'S CRIME ACADEMY

CLASSES IN KIDNAPPING

A BOOK THIS FUNNY
SHOULD BE
AGAINST THE LAW!

FROM THE
BEST-SELLING
AUTHOR OF
HORRIBLE HISTORIES

TERRY DEARY

Illustrated by John Kelly

SCHOLASTIC

This book is dedicated to the thousands of poor people who suffered and died in the workhouses of Queen Victoria. It is in memory of John Wells, who uncovered the dreadful scenes in Andover Workhouse in 1845 where poor people were set to grind bones. As John reported . . .

"I have seen the men chew the bones and break them to pick the fat and gristle out. The men were very glad to get hold of them. They were so hungry."

First published in the UK in 2009 by Scholastic Children's Books
An imprint of Scholastic Ltd
Euston House, 24 Eversholt Street
London, NW1 1DB, UK
Registered office: Westfield Road, Southam, Warwickshire, CV47 0RA
SCHOLASTIC and associated logos are trademarks and/or registered trademarks
of Scholastic Inc.

ISBN 978 1 407 11074 5

Printed and bound in the UK by CPI Mackays, Chatham, ME5 8TD
Papers used by Scholastic Children's Books are made
from wood grown in sustainable forests.

1 3 5 7 9 10 8 6 4 2

www.scholastic.co.uk/zone

CONTENTS

Before word

The Queen is dead. "Long live the King", as they say. Who says? I don't know, but it was a clever thing to say. You'll have read the reports in the newspapers. The old queen had some strange ideas. . .

Saturday 2 February 1901

The Wildpool Daily News

QUEEN: CORPSE TO COFFIN!

THE LATE QUEEN VICTORIA will be buried at Windsor Great Park today. (For our Wildpool readers we should explain that Windsor is near London.)

THE QUEEN said she wanted to be lifted into her coffin by her sons and so she was. Our Wildpool Special Royal reporter explains that she said this *before* she died.

SHE ALSO SAID (before she died) that she hated black clothes at funerals, so London was decorated in purple and white for the event.

THE MAYOR OF WILDPOOL, Sir Peter Puddle, said that Wildpool should be decorated in purple and white too. Nobody agreed with him so it never happened. As his wife

Cont.

said, "Queen Victoria never came to Wildpool so why should we care?"

THE QUEEN'S CORPSE was dressed in a white wedding dress – not the dress she wore for her wedding to Prince Albert, of course. She had grown much too fat for that.

OUR SPECIAL ROYAL reporter telephoned to say that when she was laid to rest it began to snow.

VICTORIA HAD REIGNED for sixty-three years, seven months and two days – the longest of any British ruler. (Oddly, as she was only five foot tall, she was also the shortest of any British ruler.)

THERE WERE EIGHT attempts to kill her in those sixty-three years. None of them harmed her, though Robert Pate crushed her bonnet when he struck her with his walking cane in 1850. Pate was mad. And the queen wasn't very pleased either.

IN THE END that great assassin "Old Age" got her. She left nine children and forty-two grandchildren – many of whom are kings and queens across Europe.

SHE WILL BE BURIED next to her husband, who died forty years ago, so he'll be a bit mouldy now.

THE CROWN PASSES to Prince Edward, who has only been waiting fifty-nine years to get it.

The very moment Old Queen Victoria popped her clogs, Prince Edward became King Edward. So the country and the Empire are never without a king or queen. Not even for a second.

Here's a strange thing . . . no one can tell me WHY.

What use has a king or queen ever been to us poor people? Does anybody know? Don't get me started on the subject of the rich and the rotten who rule us.

No, instead I want to tell you a more remarkable story. You see the mayor's wife said, "Queen Victoria never came to Wildpool."

The mayor's wife was quite right.

But the mayor's wife was also quite wrong.

I know. I was there at the time. There in Wildpool back in March 1837. The story has been a secret for all these years. But now I am going to let you in on it.

Mr X

18 March 1901

Chapter 1

SHADOWS AND SHEEP-HEADS

Monday 12th March 1837

The girl walked the dim streets of Wildpool. Gas lamps glowed with a silver-green light and made her pale, thin face look sickly. Her worried eyes flickered like butterflies in a bowl.

There was no one on the streets to help her. It was near midnight and even the drinkers from the ale-houses had rolled and reeled, lurched and lumbered, bumbled and blundered, bobbled and hobbled, staggered and stumbled, tottered and tumbled home.

Stray dogs played and cats ratted and bats batted . . .

at least I think that's what bats do.

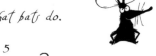

The girl looked round quickly. Something vanished into the shadow of a doorway. It was the shadow of a shadow. She looked up the steep street, Sea Road, and towards Wildpool High Street at the top. Another quarter of a mile and she would be safe.

But anything can happen in a quarter of a mile. They could still catch her and dispatch her. She pulled her shawl over her fair curly hair and hurried up the cobbles, slippery in the damp night air.

The clock on the town hall chimed the three-quarter hour. *Bing-bong, bing-bong, bing-bong. . .*

It was quarter to midnight. She had fifteen minutes to reach safety. And a lot can happen in fifteen minutes . . . some people can eat twenty pork pies in fifteen minutes.

Gas lamps did not glow at all in the dark alleys that ran between the back yards of the rows of houses to her left. She stopped at the corner of the first street and looked into the grim gloom of the alley that ran at the back of Fulwell Street. She heard an eerie creaking sound, a slosh and a panting breath of something huge and hairy. . .

All right, all right! You are right. You can't HEAR if something is hairy. It sounded huge and the girl imagined it would be hairy. In fact I once had a history teacher

who breathed like a bull but was quite bald. Bald and ugly. Apart from that she was quite a nice teacher.

There was a sharp clink of metal on the cobbles; then it started again.

Creak, slosh, pant, clink.

And the smell. The sour smell of the back house. A fat rat ran out of the alley. Not even a rat could stand that smell.

Creak, slosh, pant, clink.

She looked over her shoulder again. The shadow disappeared into the next dark doorway. Only one shadow. There should have been two.

Creak, slosh, pant, clink.

The sounds from the back alley were coming closer and looming into the light of the gas lamps on the front street.

A large hairy horse appeared first. Then the cart. And finally the two men. The night soil men. They looked up and smiled at her.

One man bent down and lifted the wooden flaps in the back yard walls. *Creak.* The other man thrust a shovel into the gap and scooped out the ashes and the human filth that had been left in the back house.

They loaded the foul mix of human waste and ashes on to the muck cart. *Slosh!*

The horse strained in its shafts to move on to the next back house flap. *Pant!*

It's hooves struck the damp cobbles. *Clink!*

The men reached the last house on the corner and stopped. "Evening, lass," the shorter one said. "Want a stick?"

She looked over her shoulder. There were a hundred shadows on the street but none were moving now. So long as she stayed with the night soil men no one could touch her.

"Why would I want a stick?" she asked.

The taller soil man shook his head. "Kids these days!" He rested on the horse and said, "You take a

8

long stick. You poke it in the back of our cart, and you get a lot of very smelly stuff on the end."

"I see," the girl said . . . though she didn't.

The shorter night soil man put in, "Then you take the stick up to the posh houses – somewhere like South Drive – and you wipe the stick on the door handles. When the posh folk come home and try to open the door. . ."

No one has played this game for years. It's sad the way these old sports die out, isn't it? Of course I wouldn't want you going out and trying this for yourself! Oh, dear, no! After all you may pick on MY door handle! Can you just forget I told you that story of the soil cart and the sticks? Thank you.

"Yes! I understand," the girl said quickly. "But I haven't time for games at the moment. I need to get to the police station on the High Street."

The men nodded. "We'll give you a ride for a hundred yards on the cart!" the little man offered, and he stretched out his hands to lift her up.

"No!" she said quickly . . . even in the dim gas-light those hands looked crusted with something unspeakable. "I'd rather walk, thanks."

9

The men nodded and turned the horse into the steep Sea Road. The horse grunted and heaved at its load. They reached the next back alley and turned into it. "Goodnight, miss," the shorter night soil man said.

The girl looked over her shoulder. The shadow was hiding in the shadow of a lamp post. But at least she was another hundred yards nearer to safety. Only three hundred to go. Suddenly, the sharp clack of running feet could be heard coming along the dark alley. The night soil men looked at one another in horror. "They're on to us!" the shorter one croaked. He let go of the reins of the horse and started to run up the hill.

A police whistle blew. The first set of footsteps had an echo. Another pair of police boots were also coming down the hill. A policeman as thin as a cucumber, with a moustache like a white bootlace, skidded to a halt. He grasped the shorter night soil man by the shoulder. "Pooh!" he cried.

Out of the dark alley came the policeman's partner – a constable as round as the moon with a face as red as Mars. He huffed to a halt.

"I arrest . . . you in the name . . . of Wildpool . . . police service. . ." he managed to say. It was a chilly

evening but the constables were sweating in their navy woollen uniforms. "Put your handcuffs on them, Constable Liddle."

"I don't have my handcuffs, Constable Larch," his thin partner said quietly. He lifted his tall top hat and mopped the sweat on his bony face and thin grey hair. "I left them in the drawer back at the station."

Larch groaned, unsure what to do. He pulled out his printed orders for the night.

WILDPOOL POLICE FORCE

Date: 12th March 1837

Orders for Night Patrol.

Proceed to Sea Road and Fulwell Street, Wildpool. Patrol the back alleys that run off Sea Road. Be careful not to be seen by anyone. Seek out and arrest the men who are emptying the night soil boxes. Lock them in the police station cell. Take them to court tomorrow morning – after you have given them a bath. (And you will probably need a bath yourselves.)

Police Inspector Beadle

Larch glared at him. "Says nothing here about forgetting handcuffs."

The taller night soil man grinned. "You'll just have to let us go then, officer!"

Larch scowled. "We'll just have to hit you over the head with our truncheons and carry you up to the police station in the back of your cart."

"No!" squawked the taller night soil man. "We'll come quietly. Honest!"

"If you were honest you wouldn't be stealing the night soil," Constable Larch grumbled. "Take them to the station, Liddle."

"Me? What about you?" the thin policeman whined.

"I'm arresting the horse and cart." He turned to the horse. "Now, are you going to come quietly too? Or do I have to use my truncheon on you?"

"Neigh," the horse replied.

This was meant to be a JOKE. It wasn't a very good joke but Constable Larch was a policeman not a Music Hall comic. He wasn't even a very good policeman. But trust me, he would NEVER use his truncheon on a horse. He would use a Pony Club.

Hah! Get it? Maybe not. Just another joke. An even worse one than Constable Larch's some might say.

They all began to march up the steep street towards the police station. The girl trotted alongside them. She was safe now. The shadows couldn't get her while she was with the Wildpool police force. Constable Larch held his black wooden truncheon in his fat paw. She smiled.

"What have the night soil men done?" she asked.

"Stolen the night soil," Larch told her as he struggled to lead the awkward horse up the hill.

"It's their job to empty the back houses. How could they steal something worthless?"

"They sell it to the farmers. The farmers spread it on their fields as manure. It's a good trade in the springtime, you know. And spring's not far away now. The real night soil men are very upset that these two have pilfered their poo. But we have cracked the crime and caught the thieves red-handed."

"*Red*-handed?" the girl said, remembering the hand that tried to lift her on the cart.

"You know what I mean," Constable Larch said.

"Ah, here we are," he said as they turned at the top of the steep street and into the High Street. The police station stood fifty yards to their left. A gas lamp glowed in a blue glass bowl that had the word *Police* painted on in white.

The girl turned and looked back down Sea Road. The gas lamps made a necklace of light that ran down to join the rows of lights in the shipyards on the river. The furnace at the glass factory made the low, cold clouds glow a dirty red. A boy stood in the middle of Sea Road, staring up at her. He'd come out of the shadows now. Defeated.

The thin girl gave a thinner smile. "Yess-ss!" she hissed. She looked towards the large house that stood next to the police station.

A sign hung on the gate.

MASTER CROOK'S CRIME ACADEMY

Tuition for the children of the poor to help them stay out of prison.

She would step through the gateway, walk ten paces across the garden, past the wind-withered tree, and enter the school. Then she would be safe. Then she would have won.

She turned to the policemen. "Goodnight, officers!" she cried cheerfully.

"Evening all," the policemen cried.

The shorter fake night soil man stopped and turned to her. "You don't know anyone wants to buy this load of night soil, do you?"

She shook her head.

"Oh, just it's a shame to see it go to waste," the man sighed and trudged under the blue light and into the station.

The girl gave one last look over her shoulder. The boy stood, helpless, at the corner of Sea Road and High Street. She wiggled her fingers at him in a cruel wave.

The town hall clock started to chime midnight. *Bing-bong, bing-bong, bing-bong, bing-bong. Donnnng! Donnnng! Donnnng!*

She stepped between the gateposts of Master Crook's Crime Academy . . . *Donnnng!* . . . and two

things happened. She suddenly wondered what happened to the boy's partner.

Donnnng! Why weren't there *two* of them at the street corner?

And then a large, rough sack was thrown over her head.

Donnnng! She breathed in to scream and the dust of the sack choked her. *Donnnng!* Before she could let out a yell, a strong hand clamped over her mouth and pressed the rough sack over her face.

Donnnng! She struggled but she knew it was useless.

The dust of the sack soaked up her tears.

Donnnng!

They weren't tears of fear or pity. They were tears of rage. Rage at knowing they'd got the sack from the sheep-head shop on Harrow Lane . . . she could tell by the smell.

Donnnng! But most of all, rage at knowing they had tricked her.

Donnnng! She was a very bad loser.

Donnnng!

Chapter 2

WOOFS AND WATERLOO

Tuesday 13th March 1837

The poster had been printed in a hurry and the ink had run a little bit. But the people of Wildpool crowded round it.

PUBLIC MEETING

MONEY TALKS
Gold talks loudest!

There will be a meeting in the town hall
On Tuesday 13th March at ten a.m.
Mayor Oswald Twistle will make some important announcements
About the FUTURE of Wildpool Town
And a SECRET royal visit

The beggar (who usually sat on the corner of the High Street) sighed and said, "I bet it means trouble for us."

The woman who owned the hat shop squinted at him. "How can you read that notice? You're supposed to be blind. I give you pennies to feed your poor little guide dog – the one with the waggly tail!"

The beggar shrugged. "This is one of my good days. I can see quite well on my good days."

"Oh! I hope my money goes to buy food for your poor little dog," she snapped.

"I buy it the best meat the butcher has in his shop and I cook it till it's perfect," the beggar said, licking his lips.

"And does your little woofy-woofy with the waggly tail like it?"

"No, but I do."

"You?"

"Yes, *I* eat it."

"What does the woofy with the waggly tail eat?"

"Nothing. It's a *toy* dog, you see," the beggar said and lifted it up for the hat-seller to see. The black button eyes stared at her like windows in an empty house. The shiny black nose was painted wood. The cute red tongue was felt and the teeth had once belonged to a dinosaur.

Don't worry, the dinosaur was dead and didn't need the teeth. The blind beggar had seen them in a museum and had borrowed them to make his toy guide dog. It was a very small dinosaur and the teeth were a bit grey. The dog now had a very cute smile. Cute but grey.

The hat-seller shook her head and her big bonnet waggled like a dog's waggly tail. "I was sure the little woofy wagged its tail every time it saw me!"

"That's because of the bit of string," the beggar explained, "fastened to my ear. I waggled my ear and the tail wagged. My ears always waggled because I was pleased to see you, of course."

"Because you admire my fair face and golden hair?" she giggled.

"No. Because you always throw a sixpence in my cap."

What he really wanted to say was, "Because you are daft as a two-foot brush." And she was. Even YOU would not have been fooled by the dog with the waggly tail. It was the big red wheels on the paws that gave it away.

He looked up. "Now, if I wasn't blind I would say the town hall clock is just about to strike ten and the

meeting will be starting soon. Better get along."

He put the dog down and pushed it along on its wheels with one hand while waving a white stick with the other. Sure enough the clock began to strike. *Bing, bong. . .*

Oh, I'm sure you know the rest. Just finish it off in your head. The chimes bonged to ten . . . if you are not very good at counting then that is one bong for each finger. Unless you are an earthworm, in which case you have a problem, or a centipede in which case you have an even bigger problem.

The beggar and the hat-seller stepped into the town hall. Mayor Twistle was very proud of his town hall. It looked a little like a Greek temple – and when Mayor Twistle looked in the mirror he saw a Greek god. Not a lot of Greek gods wear gold-rimmed spectacles, as you will know, or fine black suits. And they didn't have neat little beards either. But Mayor Twistle didn't see what the rest of the world saw – a man who was taller than a gnome . . . but only just.

None of us look in a mirror and see what the rest of the world sees.

Twistle's temple was fine. Tall columns painted gold held up a ceiling with a painting of gods having a picnic with lots of colourful fruit. At one end stood a platform where people stood to make speeches – it was quite a high platform because as you know, Mayor Oswald Twistle was a very small man.

The *bings* had finished *bonging* but the mayor had not appeared yet. He liked to keep his people waiting. He liked everyone to be in their places before he and his wife made a grand entrance. He *hated* anyone turning up late.

Behind the fine oak door he practised his speech one last time. "Mimble orrible," he said. "Mimble *orrible*?"

Bing, bong! Bing, bong. . .

The chimes sounded in Master Crook's Crime Academy. The class was restless and didn't notice the time.

At the front of the class stood their teacher, Samuel Dreep, who *did* notice the time. His gooseberry-green eyes seemed to glow. His fingers rippled like raindrops on a window pane when he talked. When he smiled his ivory teeth shone under his thin, dark moustache.

This morning, the class seemed sulky and angry. Mr

Dreep was pleased. This was a class that really *cared* about their homework. When they got it *wrong* it only made them stubborn. *Next* time they'd pass the test.

"Now, class, I need to leave you to go to a meeting in the town hall," the teacher said.

A boy with hair as wild as a dandelion, but as dark as the hold of a Wildpool coal ship, spoke up. "Is it about our next crime, Mr Dreep?"

"It may be, Smiff. I think there is a terrible wrong coming to the poor people of Wildpool," the teacher said.

A girl with a face as plain as a bag of white flour spoke up. "And, where there is a wrong, it is Master Crook's job to put it right."

"Correct, Nancy."

Nancy was a large girl with a kind face. Not at all the sort you would expect to find in a school for villains. A thin girl with fair curly hair and a face as fierce as a fox sneered. "Ooooh! *Correct*, Nancy. Well done, Nancy. Teacher's *pet* Nancy!"

Mr Dreep spoke sharply. "I know you are in one of your bad moods, Alice," he said. "But we do *not* bully our friends in Master Crook's Crime Academy."

"Hah! Who says? You says?" Alice snorted.

Mr Dreep went across to the wall and tapped a sheet of paper that was pinned there. "Rule ten, Alice . . . the top rule."

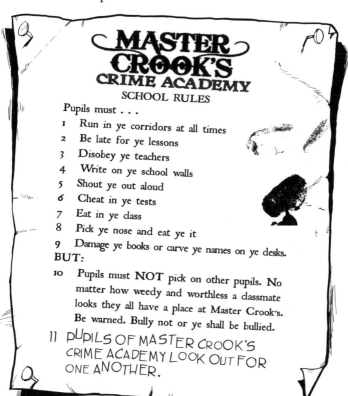

MASTER CROOK'S CRIME ACADEMY
SCHOOL RULES

Pupils must . . .

1 Run in ye corridors at all times
2 Be late for ye lessons
3 Disobey ye teachers
4 Write on ye school walls
5 Shout ye out aloud
6 Cheat in ye tests
7 Eat in ye class
8 Pick ye nose and eat ye it
9 Damage ye books or carve ye names on ye desks.

BUT:

10 Pupils must **NOT** pick on other pupils. No matter how weedy and worthless a classmate looks they all have a place at Master Crook's. Be warned. Bully not or ye shall be bullied.

11 PUPILS OF MASTER CROOK'S CRIME ACADEMY LOOK OUT FOR ONE ANOTHER.

Alice pouted. "If it's the top rule then why is it number ten? Eh?"

Mr Dreep ignored her. "While I am out I will leave you in the care of the greatest expert in kidnapping in this country."

The class snapped to attention. A new guest teacher was always exciting.

Mr Dreep marched to the door and opened it. "Come in, Miss Friday!"

A small, tubby woman waddled into the classroom. She had a face like a polished apple.

I mean, of course, a rosy apple. If you said, "Ooooh! A green apple, was it?" then you are either being stupid or awkward. Stop it at once. I am trying to tell a story here and I don't need smarty-socks like you making silly remarks. Now, can I get on? Thank you.

Mr Dreep checked his watch and went on. "Sorry, Miss Friday, I don't have time to stay and introduce you to the class. I really *have* to get to this meeting."

"Don't worry, Mr Dreep. Leave them with me," the woman said. She spoke as if she came from the south of the country.

Or, if like me you are from the north of our noble country, you could say she spoke as if she came from

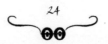

the sarf uv afr cantry. You'd be right. She was from the dark and dismal streets of London.

Dreep gave a small bow, pulled on his gloves and wrapped a red-and-white striped scarf around his neck. He left.

Miss Friday looked around the room. "Nice place you have here," she said. And it was true. The ceilings were high and decorated with plaster angels. The large windows looked out over the river and the hills to the north.

Master Crook's Crime Academy was in a house that had once been the home of a grand family. But as the shipyards grew, and the slums spread up the hill from the riverside, the rich moved out. The rich escaped the terrible disease they called cholera when it struck in 1831.

You do not want to know how hideously painful cholera was. How it spread through dirty water, how the victims were sick until they turned blue and died, how the people that nursed them died too. So I won't tell you.

And Master Crook moved in. He had opened his Crime Academy just two months before in January 1837.

"I am Miss Ruby Friday," the woman said. "Tell me who you are."

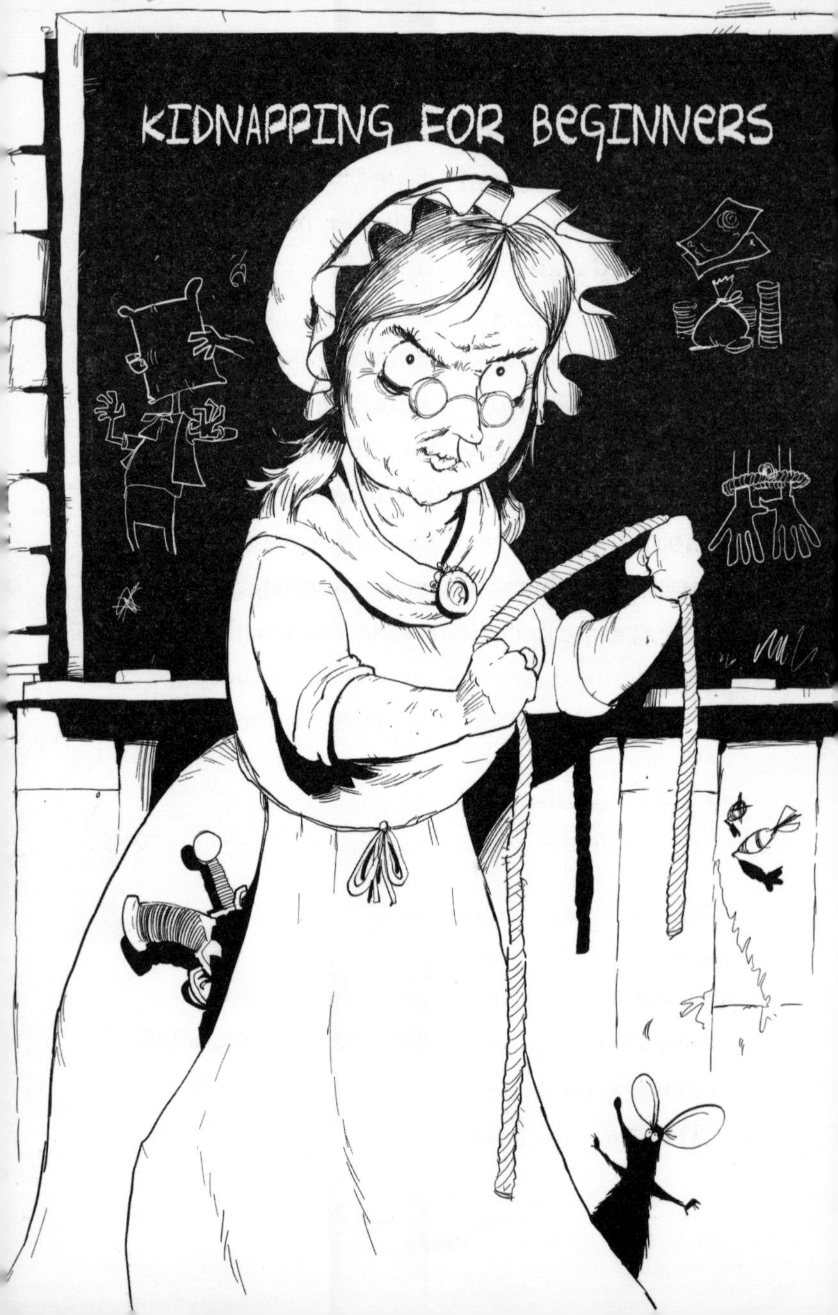
KIDNAPPING FOR BEGINNERS

And the students did. There were five of them altogether. As well as large Nancy, wild-haired Smiff and fierce Alice there was a set of thin twins – the Mixley twins, Martin and Millie.

Miss Friday looked at them. "Twins, eh? Does anyone ever Mixley you up?" the woman chuckled.

"No," Alice snapped. "Martin's the boy with the short hair and Millie's the girl with the long curls. Obvious to anyone with a bag of beans for a brain."

Ruby Friday's eyes twinkled and she smiled softly. "Oh dear, Alice. We are in a bad mood this morning. Must be because of what happened last night, is it?"

If you take a beetroot and crush it in a bowl you will get some bright red juice. Paint it on your face and that is the colour Alice turned. Some would call it "beetroot red". I'd call it "furious red".

Alice did not want to talk about last night. "So why are you the greatest expert on kidnapping in this country?" she demanded.

Ruby Friday sat at the desk. "Back in 1815 Britain was at war with France."

"This is a crime academy," Alice snapped sourly.

"We don't need no history lessons."

"I think we *all* need history lessons, Alice," Ruby Friday said quickly. "We learn lessons from the past . . . from our mistakes. Have you ever made a mistake, Alice?"

Alice snapped her mouth shut tight as a rabbit trap. Smiff smirked. "Carry on, Miss Friday."

"Britain was faced by the mighty Emperor Napoleon," the new teacher went on. "The French army met the Brits at a village called Waterloo and we all knew who was going to win."

"The British!" Martin Mixley said in his piping voice.

"No. The *French*!" Ruby Friday said. "No one could beat Emperor Napoleon and his mighty French army."

"But we did!" Millie cried.

The teacher raised a finger. "The British leader, the Duke of Wellington, sent for me. I was the British army's only hope!"

"I thought you were a kidnapper," Alice grumbled. "Now you're telling us you're a general?"

Again Miss Friday raised a finger. "I went to Paris. I kidnapped Napoleon's wife, the Empress Josephine."

The class gasped.

"We sent Napoleon a little message the night before Waterloo. Lose the battle . . . or lose your empress."

"And he lost the battle to save Josephine!" Millie Mixley cried. "That's romantic. Ahhhh!"

"See? Kidnapping isn't just for money," Ruby Friday said. "A good kidnapping can change the history of the world. And that's what we plan to do, isn't it?"

The five Master Crook students nodded . . . even angry Alice.

The Duke of Wellington went on to be Prime Minister of Britain and one of the most hated men in Britain – he loved to crush the poor people. Oh yes, he won the battle of Waterloo, of course. But he never told anyone the tale of Ruby Friday and the kidnapped Josephine. Welly was just too ashamed of his sneaky trick.

Chapter 3

RUBY AND RANSOM

"Friends!" Mayor Oswald Twistle cried. The audience looked up to see their mayor standing on the platform in the great hall of the town hall.

Lady Arabella Twistle stood next to him in a dress of finest silks. Today the colour was pink to match her nose. She always wrote her husband's speeches.

"Friends, Wildpoolians, countrymen!" the mayor went on. "Today is a mimble orrible day for Wildpool."

"What?" the crowd gasped.

"Memorable," Arabella hissed. "The word is memorable."

"Today is a memble-rabble day."

The large woman sighed. "It is a day we will never forget."

"Today is a day we will always forget!" Oswald cried. He cleared his throat. Now he had started it got easier . . . in fact it was sometimes hard to stop him. But the door at the back opened and a man with a red-and-white striped scarf stepped into the chamber. Late. Mayor Twistle looked at the young man with poison darts.

"Why is it a memorable day?" the blind beggar called out.

"Yes! Get on with it you buffoon," the latecomer shouted from the back. It was Samuel Dreep, the teacher at Master Crook's Crime Academy.

But you knew that from the red-and-white striped scarf, didn't you? You have a sharp mind. Be careful it doesn't cut its way through your skull.

"Last year," Mayor Oswald went on, "the council of Wildpool raised thirteen hundred pounds in order to build a workhouse for the town. As you know it is the fine stone building at the north end of the bridge!"

"Yes, built well away from your posh house at the south end of town," Mr Dreep jeered. The mayor ignored him.

"Last month Lady Arabella Twistle . . . my wife. . ."

"My *lovely* wife," her ladyship muttered. "Read what I wrote," she said and sat down.

". . .my *lovely* wife, became leader of the workhouse governors. This afternoon the workhouse will open its doors for the first time." He let the speech rest on the table and peered through his glasses at the curious crowd. His voice rose. "Now there is somewhere for the poor of Wildpool to be shut away, out of our sight, so we don't have to suffer their begging, their whining and their horrible smell! We won't have to bear the stinking scent of their unwashed clothes and their unpolished boots, the shame of their seatless trousers and their meatless meals, their bawling babies and shivering shoeless, clueless, useless children; their cold old codgers that can't keep their teeth and the layabout lazers who sleep in their sacks till it's time to come out and rob the rich of our hard-earned gold, and I for one have had *enough*, I say. *Enough!* And that's not all. . ."

Lady Arabella rose quickly to her feet like a hot air

balloon rises over the basket when the hot air fills it. "What my husband *means* to say," she bellowed over the top of him, "is that now there is somewhere for the poor, the sick and the old to be cared for. We want to make sure there is work for everyone and there will be lots of work in the workhouse."

"That's probably why it's called a workhouse then!" the trouble-making Dreep laughed.

Mayor Twistle jumped up and said, "Our new workhouse will be run by the overseers – Mr and Mrs Humble. A fine pair of caring people you will all agree . . . if you meet them . . . which I hope you don't . . . because if you meet them, then that means you've been locked away in the workhouse . . . and you wouldn't want that! I suppose, of course, you *could* be a visitor to the workhouse in which case you will *not* be locked away . . . and if you visit you WILL get to meet the Humbles . . . and you will see how fine they are . . . See?"

I did warn you that once the mayor got started he was hard to stop. He was a bit like a dripping tap. Have you ever had one of those? Drives you mad. The more you WANT it to stop the more it annoys you. A dripping tap can sometimes be fixed by a sharp blow from a hammer. So could Mayor Twistle I suppose.

Lady Arabella rested a hand on her husband's shoulder and pushed him into his seat. She smiled her pink smile at the puzzled people. "What this means is there is now NO excuse for the poor to clutter up the streets of Wildpool and make it look untidy. No excuse for beggars to bother the rich people like us with their pawing, clawing, grubby hands. Now we have somewhere for them to go."

The blind beggar sighed and looked at his dog. "I knew it. I said it would be bad news for us, didn't I?" The dog didn't answer.

"No one will be *forced* to go into the workhouse, of course," the mayor's wife went on.

"Can I take my dog with me?" the beggar called.

"No you CANNOT."

"Then I won't go," the beggar shrugged.

Lady Arabella's face turned a deeper shade of pink. "Then we will *force* you to go."

"Force me to go into the workhouse where no one will be forced to go?"

"Exactly!" the woman said with a grim grin.

She reached on to the table and unrolled a poster.

WILDPOOL WORKHOUSE
WELCOMES

THE POOR AND NEEDY, THE SICK AND THE OLD
MEN? ARE YOU OUT OF WORK?
COME TO THE WW AND WE'LL FIND YOU PLENTY
WOMEN? STRUGGLING TO FEED AND CLOTHE YOUR FAMILY?
BRING THEM TO WW AND WE'LL MAKE SURE YOU
ALL HAVE PLENTY OF WORK TO DO SO YOU CAN
FEED YOURSELVES! AND NO MORE WORRIES ABOUT
CLOTHES! WE GIVE YOU A UNIFORM!
We even allow mothers to see their children for an hour every Sunday!
Children? Are you an orphan? Homeless? Need a good meal?
Come to WW and work for one! It won't be the best meal you've
ever eaten – but it is better than starving.

BEFORE   AFTER

APPLY TO: WILDPOOL WORKHOUSE,
NORTH BRIDGE STREET, WILDPOOL

Lady Arabella whispered to Sir Oswald and he scurried off the stage to the door at the side. She waved in the two Wildpool policemen.

"We have here our fine police force," Lady Arabella smiled.

The two men shuffled into line. They bent their knees and bobbed down. "Evening all," they said as one.

It was morning. You know that. I know that. The policemen know that. But they hadn't practised "Morning all," so they didn't want to get it wrong and look stupid. Instead they said "Evening all" in the morning . . . and looked stupid anyway.

Mayor Twistle bounced back on to the stage. "And last night they cracked yet another major crime in our fine town! They arrested the night soil thieves *and* their horse! They can look forward to a life of hard labour in Darlham Gaol for that!"

Constable Larch lurched forward. "Ahem . . . I'm sorry, Sir Oswald, but we have just come from the courtroom. The trial has just ended. A young girl stood up in court as a witness. She said the usual soil men spent all night in the tavern before they set off to empty the privies. She said the fake soil men did a much better job! The judge sentenced them to one month of emptying the soil from the new workhouse without pay. He said Constable Liddle and I should be doing more useful things than nicking a pair of poo pinchers!"

Mayor Twistle's face twisted as if he were chewing a worm. At last he managed to smile. "Quite right – and so you shall! You have a new task. Your job is to sweep the streets of Wildpool. . ."

"Do we have to buy our own brushes?" Constable Liddle asked.

"Sweep it of the poor, the beggars and the orphans, the homeless and the old. You are going to clean up this town," the mayor said.

"But do we have to buy our own brushes?"

Mayor Twistle rolled his eyes. "No, you idiot. I *mean* you take these dreadful people and drag them off to the workhouse. No trials, no judges. Just stick them out of sight."

"No brushes?"

"No brushes."

"That's good."

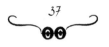

37

"Why?"

"Because I haven't got one."

Lady Twistle stepped forward again and her chubby elbow knocked the policemen to the back of the platform. "We need clean streets because at the end of this week Wildpool will have the most important visitor it has ever had in its proud history!"

"Who's that then?" Samuel Dreep shouted.

"Someone so important that it has to be a secret!" Lady Arabella said with a smug smile.

"The king?" a woman with a glass eye and an umbrella cried.

I know what you are going to say. You are thinking that she could have worn an eye patch instead of a glass eye. But she didn't have any black material to make an eye patch – she'd used it all up to make the umbrella. She had very little money. But don't weep for the woman – her glass eye never cried for her, so why should you?

"Don't be daft – King William's too sick to leave London."

"Oh, well, if it's not the king I won't get me flags out," the woman sighed.

"This is a private visit . . . arranged by Sir Oswald and myself," Lady Twistle said. "But our guest will travel through the streets and we don't want it cluttered with beggars, do we?"

"Bad news for me," the blind beggar sighed.

Samuel Dreep twirled his curled moustache. "Ah, but a chance for someone to have a little fun, I think."

He chuckled. He chuckled all the way back to Master Crook's Crime Academy.

Ruby Friday looked at the class. "Now, Mr Dreep gave you some homework last night. Tell me how you got on."

Millie Mixley raised her pale hand as if she were in school. "Please, miss, the homework was this: Alice had to walk from the shipyards on the riverside, up the hill up to Master Crook's Crime Academy. Two of us had to kidnap her before she got here . . . but Alice didn't know *which* two."

Alice glared at the girl. "I could have guessed it would be sneaky Smiff and tough Nancy Turnip."

Ruby nodded. "And you all failed dreadfully, didn't you, Smiff?"

"No!" the rough-haired boy cried. "I think not! Alice lost. We got her!"

"You cheated," Alice spat.

Smiff raised his nose in the air. "School rule number six. Cheat in tests. I prefer to say we had a clever plan and it worked."

"Tell me," Ruby said softly.

Smiff began. "I hid on the corner of Garth Court because you can see all the streets that lead from the shipyards. I just had to wait for Alice to appear and follow her."

Alice blew out her cheeks and made the sound of a snorting pig. "I saw you. You were hopeless. You tried to hide in the shadows. But I *saw* you."

Smiff gave that annoying smirk. "You were meant to."

"What?"

"You were *meant* to see me. You tried dodging into back alleys. Then you met the night soil men. The policemen arrested them and you went along with them all the way to the gates of the Crime Academy.

40

All the time you thought you were safe because you could see me."

"And I was," Alice argued.

"But Nancy was waiting behind the gatepost of the Crime Academy. *She* got you!"

"Yeah, with a smelly sack from the sheep-head shop. There was no need for *that*," Alice snarled. "I had to wash my hair to get the smell out."

"First time this year, was it?" Smiff jeered.

Alice made her fists into tight balls and half rose. Ruby Friday spoke quickly, "But you *failed*, Smiff."

Alice froze. "Did he?"

Smiff blinked. "I think not . . . er . . . did I?"

"Yes! Alice *saw* you."

"That was part of the plan! She was so busy looking at me she never saw Nancy."

The old teacher shook her head. "If this had been a real kidnapping, for money, what would you do next?"

"Please, miss," Martin Mixley put in. "We would write out a ransom note. We tried some in class yesterday." He showed it to Ruby Friday.

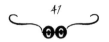

> DEAR MASTER CROOK,
>
> WE HAVE TAKEN YOUR GIRL, ALICE WHITE, PRISONER. WE WILL NOT HARM HER IF YOU PAY US FIFTY POUNDS IN GOLD.
>
> PUT THE GOLD IN A SACK AND LEAVE IT BEHIND THE OAK TREE WHERE THE GREAT NORTH ROAD CROSSES THE WILDPOOL TO WISHINGTON RAILWAY LINE.
>
> IF YOU DO NOT DO THIS I WILL NOT TELL YOU WHAT WE WILL DO TO ALICE. IT IS SO HORRIBLE YOU WOULD NOT WANT TO KNOW SO I WILL NOT TELL YOU. JUST LEAVE THE GOLD OR ELSE.
>
> A FRIEND

Millie Mixley explained. "The note says what we want in return for the victim. We collect the ransom and we're rich!"

Ruby Friday looked at Alice. "Suppose these kidnappers had sold you back to Master Crook for fifty pounds. . ."

"I'm worth at least a hundred," Alice grumbled.

"Very well, a hundred pounds," Miss Friday said calmly. "They get their hundred pounds. Then they set you free. What would you do, Alice?" the woman asked.

"Get my own back on Smiff!" Alice said with a fierce grin.

"And how would you know it was Smiff to blame?"

Alice frowned. "Cos I *saw* him!"

"Exactly!" Ruby Friday nodded. "Holy crumpets . . . excuse my bad language. A kidnapper must *never* let their victim see their face!" She turned to Smiff. "Alice *saw* you. She would tell the police. The police would arrest you and you'd spend the rest of your life in Darlham Gaol – that's if they didn't hang you."

Alice was smiling sweetly now.

Well, as sweetly as a bull terrier could ever smile – the sort of smile the terrier has when it is guarding a house and it sees a burglar's leg appear through a window. A sweet smile . . . but not a nice smile.

"Yeah! I'd come and visit you, Smiffy. Heh! You loser!"

"If you came to visit I'd *beg* them to hang me," he muttered.

Ruby Friday clapped her hands. "So that's our first lesson in kidnapping! We need to work on the art of *disguise*."

The door opened and Mr Dreep stepped in. "Sorry to interrupt your lesson, Miss Friday, but it is lunch time now . . . and I need to tell the class about Master

Crook's Crime Academy's first school trip."

"Somewhere nice?" the Mixley twins cried.

"The mayor says so," Mr Dreep shrugged.

"But the mayor tells lies," Nancy said quietly. "The mayor tells terrible lies."

The March day was cold and gloomy. But not as gloomy as the gloomy room in the Wildpool police station. Inspector Beadle sat behind his desk and shook his head. This was a great effort. It was a very large head. It sat on an even larger body. That body wasn't as wide as a rhino or as heavy as a hippo. But you wouldn't want to bump into it when you were running to catch a bus . . . or catch a cold . . . or whatever else you run to catch.

"It has not been a good day for Wildpool police," Beadle said and his voice rumbled till the gas lamp on the ceiling trembled.

Constables Liddle and Larch trembled too. They twisted their top hats in their hands and looked at the floor.

"The night soil thieves went free," the inspector went on.

"And the horse," Liddle added. "Did you know they didn't even let the horse into the court room?

He was properly arrested and everything! Look!" He
waved the paper at the inspector.

WILDPOOL POLICE FORCE
Charge Sheet

Arresting officer/s:	Liddle and Larch
Date of arrest:	13th March 1837
Place of arrest:	Fulwell Street
Time of arrest*:	ten minutes past midnight
Accused:	Edward (Ned) Carthorse
For the crime of	feloniously aiding the filching of foul filth

Signed   PC Septimus Liddle (PC 01)
PC Archibald Larch (PC 02)

*Note: No person may be held for more than twenty-four hours
without being charged with a crime. This law goes back to 1215

Notes: The law goes back to 12:15, but we arrested this horse five
minutes before that, at 12:10, so it doesn't count. We can keep him as
long as we like, or until we run out of hay

Inspector Beadle shook his huge head sadly. "Mayor Twistle was not pleased. In fact, Mayor Twistle said he would like *you* to spend a few years in Darlham Gaol."

"It wasn't our fault!" Larch wailed and his chins shook as if he were about to cry. "*You* gave us the order."

Somewhere in the folds of fat, Inspector Beadle's mouth may have smiled. "Yes, I did, didn't I?" He spread his hands, each one as large as a night soil shovel . . . only cleaner. "But now you have a chance to make Mayor Twistle a very happy man and save your jobs. All you have to do is fill up his new workhouse on North Bridge Street."

The constables nodded. "How do we do that, sir?"

Inspector Beadle pointed to the Wildpool map on the wall. "Down by the river there is a square of houses. It's called Garth Court."

"Ooooh!" Liddle gasped. "We never go in there! It's dark! Even on a sunny day it's dark and damp."

"And smelly," Larch added.

"And that's where the cholera lives. You turn blue,

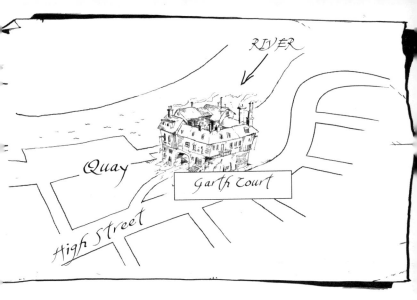

you know, before you die," Liddle moaned. "I don't want to turn blue!"

"I don't want to die!" his partner added.

Inspector Beadle leaned forward and glared. "You are two old town watchmen. We gave you jobs in the new police force. If we sack you then you will have no jobs. Where will you end up? In the workhouse. You either fill the new workhouse with the poor people of Garth Court or you end up there yourselves."

Larch dared to look up. "Oh, that's not so bad, then! Mayor Twistle said it's a lovely place!"

Inspector Beadle's eyes were cold and hard as winter. "Mayor Twistle lied."

Chapter 4

PENCE AND PAUPERS

Wildpool workhouse was grey. Grey as a tombstone. Grey stone walls, grey stone floors and the cheap, grey-stained glass let in grey light from a grey sky.

A man and a woman looked at the rows of empty seats in the great hall and dreamed. "These seats will soon be full, Angela."

"Amelia."

"What?" the man asked and scratched his thick, dark, greasy hair that sat low on thick eyebrows that met in the middle. His eyes were too close together, his nose too small and his mouth too wide. A mouth full of grey teeth like tombstones. He may have been thirty

years old. He may have been thirty thousand. It's hard to tell the age of someone who shares his face with a cave man.

"My name is Amelia. We agreed."

"I forgot, my sweetness," he sighed.

"You would forget your own name if it wasn't stitched on to the front of your uniform," she smiled. She had a lovely smile, rather like a gorilla with a bunch of bananas. Her face was as rough as the workhouse walls, scarred with old diseases, her sharp eyes like silver beads and her needle nose as dangerous as a dagger.

He looked at the label. "Mr Humble – Overseer."

"That's right. You are Harry Humble and I am Amelia Humble. But, when we are in here, I will call you Mr Humble and you will call me Mrs Humble. Understand, my duckling?"

"Yes, my sweetness."

"Now . . . Hengist, I mean Harry, I mean Mr Humble . . . what were you saying?"

He scratched his dark hair again, pulled something out and popped it in his mouth where he crunched it with tombstone teeth. "I forget, sweetness."

49

"You were saying, this room will soon be full of the poor people of Wildpool."

"I just said that!" he cried. "Yes, I did . . . and the more poor people we have in here the more money we are paid." He chuckled and rubbed his rough hands together.

"We are paid six pence a day for every pauper we have," the woman who called herself Amelia Humble said. "We feed them for three pence a day. The other three pence goes in our pocket, my duckling."

"Twenty-one pence a week for every pauper. A hundred paupers and we have twenty-one hundred pence a week . . . that's a hundred and seventy-five shillings . . . that's eight pounds fifteen shillings a week . . . every week!"

He scribbled it on some paper with a sharp new pencil.

3 PENCE x 7 DAYS = 21 PENCE

21 PENCE x 100 PAUPERS = 2100 PENCE

2100 PENCE DIVIDED BY 12 = 175 SHILLINGS

175 SHILLINGS DIVIDED BY 20 = 8 POUNDS AND 15 SHILLINGS LEFT OVER.

TOTAL: 8 POUNDS AND 15 SHILLINGS A WEEK

TOTAL EVERY YEAR: 8 POUNDS AND 15 SHILLINGS TIMES 52 = A LOT!

Like many wicked and greedy people the man was not exactly clever. But when it came to money he had a brain like one of those new adding machines. But trust me, in every other way the man who called himself Harry Humble was stupid.

"We'll be the richest people in Wildpool before the summer comes!" Mrs Humble crowed.

"Ah, my sweetness, we will have to take care of the paupers," her husband warned.

"Why is that my duckling?"

"Well . . . if one of them dies we will lose . . . erm. . ." He scribbled again.

3 PENCE x 7 DAYS = 21 PENCE
21 PENCE x 52 WEEKS = 1092 PENCE
1092 PENCE DIVIDED BY 12 = 91 SHILLINGS
91 SHILLINGS DIVIDED BY 20 = 4 POUNDS AND 11 SHILLINGS LEFT OVER.

"There you are, Angela. . ."

"Amelia or Mrs Humble, duckling."

"There you are, *Mrs Humble*. If a pauper dies

we lose four pounds and eleven shillings every year!"

The woman's silver eyes glittered. "Oh, no. If a pauper *dies* we keep on taking the six pence a day for them. But we stop paying the three pence for their food – dead paupers eat less. . . Heh! Heh!"

"Oh, very funny, Mrs Humble."

"Instead of *losing* four pounds and eleven shillings we get *another* four pounds and eleven shillings! A dead pauper makes us nine pounds and two shillings every year!"

"Ah, yes, my sweet, but we have to pay the cost of the funeral. They can cost almost a pound these days," he reminded her.

She shook her head slowly. "No funeral. We are near the bridge. We wrap up the pauper in a sheet with some stones. When the workhouse is asleep we slip out and drop the body off the bridge and into the river. No one will ever know."

"That's good, that is, Mrs Humble," the man said. "I could kiss you on your clever little nose."

"And so you shall, sweetness, after we have finished

the menu for the week. Mayor Twistle and his royal guest will want to see it. Here we go, almost finished."

She wrote the last figures in the last day and looked at it proudly.

WILDPOOL WORKHOUSE DIETARY

	THE GENERAL DIETARY								AGED, INFIRM AND SICK DIETARY								
	Breakfast		Dinner				Supper		Breakfast		Dinner				Supper		
															Men	Men & Wom.	
	Bread oz.	Gruel pints.	Beef oz.	Soup pints.	Suet Pud oz.	Potatoes lb.	Cheese oz.	Broth pints.	Bread oz.	Gruel pints.	Beef or Mutton	Potatoes lb.	Soup pints.	Rice Pud oz.	Cheese oz.	Broth pints.	Women
MONDAY	14	1.5	5	~	~	1	~	1.5	10	1.5	5	1	~	~	~	1.5	
TUESDAY	14	1.5	~	1.5	~	~	2	~	10	1.5	~	~	1.5	~	2	~	Tea to be made by the Matron, and one Pint to be given to each person twice a day with Bread & Butter, in Lieu of Gruel or Broth
WEDNESDAY	14	1.5	5	~	~	1	~	1.5	10	1.5	5	1	~	~	~	1.5	
THURSDAY	14	1.5	~	1.5	~	~	2	~	10	1.5	~	~	1.5	~	~	1.5	
FRIDAY	8	1.5	~	~	14	~	2	~	10	1.5	~	~	1.5	~	2	~	
SATURDAY	14	1.5	5	~	~	1	~	1.5	10	1.5	5	1	~	10	2	~	
SUNDAY	14	1.5	~	1.5	~	~	2	~	10	1.5	5	1	~	~	~	1.5	

"Oh, those lucky, lucky paupers," Mrs Humble sighed.

"And lucky, lucky us!" her husband chuckled. "Who'd have thought we'd get such a good job so soon after coming out of prison, sweetness?"

Her voice turned as sharp as her nose. "Never mention that, duckling. Never. No one must know. No one."

In Wildpool police station, Inspector Beadle looked at the card in front of him on the desk. The prison artist had drawn the faces well. They stared out at him as real as if they were alive.

You have to remember that this was back in 1837 and photographs had not quite been invented. But a good artist can show a face BETTER than a photograph. A villain can hide their wickedness when the camera clicks. But an artist sees the lies behind the eyes and sketches them. Next time you are arrested let them take your photograph – don't let them sketch you! I offer you this priceless tip for free. I am too, too kind.

DARLHAM GAOL

Convicts: Hengist and Angela Harper

Origins: 37 Grape Street, South Banchester Town

Arrested: 11th February 1836, Darlham Town

Crime: Capturing children of the rich, stripping off their clothes, shoes and selling them to clothes shops

Judgement: One year in prison each as no children were found to be harmed

Sentence: Released 13th February 1837

He tapped the card with a finger that was as thick as a sausage. Then he placed it carefully in the drawer of his desk and locked it.

Samuel Dreep stood in front of the Wildpool workhouse gateway. It was a fine arch with heavy doors painted dark green. The walls were high. There were spikes along the tops of the walls and the gate itself. It would be as hard to escape from here as from Darlham Gaol.

The Mixley twins stood by his side. Millie's hair was now as short as her brother's. They wore the oldest clothes their mother could find – the clothes they had worn when they were penniless and before Master Crook had saved them.

"You know why I chose you?" Dreep asked. He twirled the tip of his moustache. The twins looked so frail he was worried this would be too tough a task. But their bright faces smiled up at him.

"We always do as we're told, sir," Millie said.

"If you sent Alice in here she would start a riot, and that's not what we want, sir," Martin added.

"And if you sent Smiff in here he'd spend all his

time in the punishment room in the yellow jacket . . . please, sir, what's the yellow jacket?" Millie asked.

"Ah! Workhouse rules. Anyone who makes trouble is forced to wear the yellow jacket so they are easy to spot," Samuel Dreep explained.

The twins nodded. "You'd never see us in the yellow jacket," Millie said.

Dreep leaned forward. "They will work you hard and try to starve you," he said.

"That's all right, sir, we can take it!" Martin laughed. "Last month when we were poor our mother fed us peas for dinner."

"That's good," the teacher said.

"We had one pea each," Millie sighed.

"That's bad," the teacher agreed.

"One evening I got upset," Martin put in. "I thought Millie had *two* peas!"

"But I'd taken mine and cut it in half!" she said and the twins giggled.

Millie shivered suddenly as the March wind blew in from the river. "Oh, I can't get used to having my hair cut short like Martin," she sighed. "Or the trousers."

Samuel Dreep nodded. "You too look so alike now . . . and that may help. The plan is for Martin to find out how the workhouse works . . . is there a good way to get in and out? Are the Humbles as good as Mayor Twistle says?"

"Mayor Twistle *lies*!" Millie gasped. "Nancy says so and she should know – she used to work for him!"

"Or are the Humbles really the wicked Harpers from Darlham Gaol the way Master Crook says?" Dreep went on. "Now, you have the paper and pencils?"

"Yes, sir," Martin said.

"Wrap a message round a stone and throw it over the gate if you need any help or if you can find a way out to report. Now, are you ready?"

"Yes, sir!"

"Millie, you hide round the corner. Don't let them see you."

Millie nodded and ran off.

Mr Dreep tugged at the rope that hung by the side of the gate and somewhere inside a bell rang. A minute later they heard bolts being pulled back and the new doors creaked on their new hinges. A man with a face

like an angry beetle glared out at them.

"What you want then, eh?" he said.

"Mr Humble?"

"Pleased to meet you, Mr Humble," beetle-face said.

"No, no, no," Dreep laughed. "*I'm* not Mr Humble . . . *you* are Mr Humble."

"Who says?"

"Mayor Oswald Twistle."

"Oh . . . yes! That's right. I'm Humble. Humble by name and humble by nature, Mrs Harp – er – Mrs Humble always says! What can I do for you?"

Dreep handed him a printed card.

MR SAMUEL DREEP

*Master of Education
Trained felon, malefactor, desperado,
contrabandist and conspirator)*

c/o Master Crook's Crime Academy,
High Street, Wildpool

"Look to Crook to get not took!"

"Dreep, eh?"

"This unfortunate child was found on our doorstep this morning."

"Doorstep? What were he doing there?"

"Crying."

"Yes . . . I meant. . ."

"He was left with a label around his neck. Here it is!"

To whom it may concern,

I am no longer able to feed my dear child. I am going south to look for work. I cannot send him to the workhouse because the workhouse rules say I have to go with him. If I go to the workhouse I will never find a job. So I thought Master Crook could look after him – train him so he get not took. What do you think?

Signed: his loving dad.

PS Martin is a very fussy eater and eats only the thinnest of gruel. In fact he hardly eats anything.

"Sadly Master Crook has no room in the academy. I wondered if you could break your rules and take him in without a parent?" Dreep asked.

"Hah! At sixpence a day! I'll say I can."

"Even though it's against the rules?"

"Hah! Rules was meant to be broken," beetle-faced Humble snorted.

I will call him Humble even though YOU know he is really Harper. You don't have to show how clever you are and tell me, "You got his name wrong." Don't try being clever, try being humble – after all, Harper did.

"There you are, child! You can go in here and break the rules!"

"No!" Humble squawked. "Not *my* rules! You break *my* rules and I'll beat you like a dog," he said fiercely and spit flew out on bad breath as he raged. He looked up at Samuel Dreep. "Don't worry, Mr Dreep, I'm sure he'll be very happy . . . oh, and if you find any more then bring them along. The more the merrier, we always say."

"The child is called—"

"Doesn't matter!" Humble cut in. "From now on he will be a *number* not a name." He pointed at Martin and said, "You are number one. Welcome to Wildpool's Wonderful Workhouse!"

He slammed the gate and it rang with a boom like doom.

Chapter 5

CARTS AND COPS

Wednesday 14th March 1837

Wildpool High Street was busy and bustling to the point of bursting. The washer-woman had parked her cart on the corner and blocked half of the road while she delivered clean washing and collected the dirty.

Carriages queued and wagons waited, carts collided and barrows tried to barge through. Drivers argued and shoppers smiled to see the sport. The hat-seller came to her shop door and said to the blind beggar, "It's ages since I've seen a good fight."

"I've never seen a good fight!" the blind beggar said.

"You must have done . . . sitting there," she cried.

"I'm blind. I see nothing . . . that way I don't have

to go to court as a witness," he said and he took off the dark spectacles he wore so he could get a better look. Two carters had jumped down to sort out the tangle of their wheels. They were red in the face and shouting while their dogs yapped at one another.

"Call yourself a driver? You shouldn't be allowed out on the roads."

"Call yourself a human being? You look more like a monkey to me except a monkey could drive that thing better. You drove straight into me."

"I think not, my friend."

"I'm not your friend. I don't have monkeys for friends."

"If you've bruised my tomatoes, I'll batter you."

"If you've hurt my toads, I'll splatter you."

"*Toads?* What you carrying *toads* for?"

"The old alchemist shop. He uses lots of toads in his medicines." The carter pulled one off the back of the cart and waved it under the tomato cart driver's nose. "See?"

"Aaaagggghhhh! Get it away from me. I hate them." He picked up a handful of tomatoes and started to pelt the toad cart driver. Then they started to push one another till they were both rolling in the muddy road.

The hat-seller sighed. "Not much of a fight."

"No," the blind beggar agreed and put his glasses back on. "Just a touch of toad rage."

Constable Liddle and Constable Larch stepped out of the police station and wound their way around the tangle of wagons, dogs and rats, as they read their orders for the day.

WILDPOOL POLICE FORCE

Date: 14th March 1837

Orders for Evening Patrol:

Proceed through the main streets of Wildpool

Question anyone who is begging or does not appear to be

working or is a pauper

Note their name

Accompany the persons to Wildpool workhouse on North Bridge

Street

Hand them into the custody of Mr or Mrs Humble

Then proceed to Garth Court and take everyone into custody.

Police Inspector Beadle

They stepped over the two carters who were rolling like slow slugs on the cobbles.

"C-o-p!" the hat-seller said to the beggar.

"Cop?"

"Constables On Patrol . . . we call them cops for short, see?"

"I see nothing," the beggar said.

The woman called out, "Here! Constables? Aren't you going to sort out this traffic?"

Constable Larch looked up at Constable Liddle. "Traffic? Is that part of our job?"

Liddle stroked his wispy white moustache. "Here's one of the poems the mayor wrote when he gave us the job. . ."

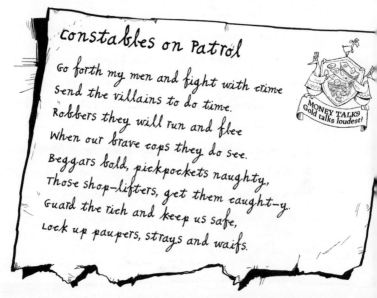

Constables on Patrol

Go forth my men and fight with crime
Send the villains to do time.
Robbers they will run and flee
When our brave cops they do see.
Beggars bold, pickpockets naughty,
Those shop-lifters, get them caught-y.
Guard the rich and keep us safe,
Lock up paupers, strays and waifs.

MONEY TALKS
Gold talks loudest!

"What's a waif?" Liddle muttered.

"A sort of biscuit I think."

"No, that's a wafer." He pushed one of the panting, struggling carters with his boot. "Excuse me, sir, are you a waif?"

The red-faced man looked up. "I don't think so."

Liddle looked at the man he was wrestling with. "What about you? A waif?"

"Yoo-hoo!"

"No, I think he said 'waif' not 'wave'."

"Sorry. No."

The constables nodded. "Thought not. Carry on, gents."

The two men helped one another to their feet and hobbled back to their carts.

"So!" the hat-seller cried. "You're not going to sort out this traffic?"

"That's not a job for policemen!" Liddle said. "Let them sort themselves out."

The woman threw her hands in the air. "The road is blocked. No one can get to my shop. No one can get to this poor blind beggar and his dog. It's costing us money."

67

Larch shrugged. The cops walked to the corner of the High Street. They stopped. They looked at one another. "Here, Liddle. Did she say what I think she said?"

"Beggar?"

"We need to arrest that man! Take him off to the Wildpool's Wonderful Waxworks."

"I think you mean workhouse, Liddle."

The tall, thin grey policeman looked at his paper. "So I do."

They turned and walked back to the beggar. "Penny for the dog?" the man said in his most pitiful voice.

"Are you begging?"

"I can see you are a clever man, spotting that, Constable. Top marks!" the beggar laughed.

"In that case I arrest you. You will accompany us to the waxworks," Liddle said. "I mean the Work-wax . . . where you will be given work to pay for your food and bed."

The man was hauled to his feet. "What about me dog?"

"Can he work?"

"No, but. . ."

"Then he can't go," Larch said, harshly.

"Don't worry, I'll look after the dear little mutt," the hat-seller said. "He can sleep on my bed every night."

I'm pleased about that. I can't stand to see animals badly treated. That lucky dog would have a warm and cosy new home and a loving owner. Of course he'd have to suffer a good bath first – he was as smelly as a sailor's sock. But afterwards he'd be dried by the fire and brushed. He would be given a name . . . dogs like that. And, of course, he would be taken for walks every day and have his wheels oiled with love . . . and oil.

"Thanks, lady!" the beggar managed to cry before he was dragged towards the Wildpool bridge and over to the workhouse.

Mrs Humble answered the bell. "What you want then, eh?" she said.

"We are very happy to deliver this unfortunate beggar to your loving care," Larch said and looked at his paper. "Er . . . Mrs Humble."

"The beggar's called *Mrs Humble*? Funny name."

"No," Liddle said. "*You* are called Mrs Humble."

69

"Am I?"

"If you are the workhouse keeper then that's your name," the policeman said with a frown.

"Ah . . . oh . . . eh . . . yes-s-s-s! That's me!" the woman said with a sharp-toothed smile.

"So you'll take this beggar?"

"What? Just *one*? Is that *it*? We can't make a living with just two! We need a hundred. I thought my friend Sir Oswald Twistle told you to sweep the streets!"

"As I told him," Liddle said, "I don't have a brush."

"But is this the best you can do? One miserable beggar?" she raged.

"I offered to bring me dog," the beggar said.

"Dogs don't count. If dogs come here, we cook them and eat them," she snarled.

"Glad I didn't bring him then!" the beggar gasped.

The woman turned her sharp nose on the constables. "We have an important visitor arriving here on Friday. We were promised a hundred paupers by then. If Sir Oswald finds you've failed he really *will* have you sweeping the streets. Sweeping the horse droppings in the High Street. Now push off and do what the mayor said."

She grabbed the beggar by the shirt and pulled him through the door.

"Excuse me!" Constable Liddle said, pulling out his notebook. "But we have to fill in the correct form."

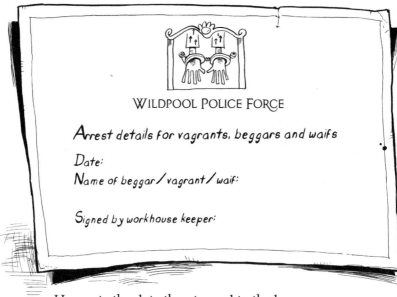

WILDPOOL POLICE FORCE

*A*rrest details for vagrants, beggars and waifs

*D*ate:

*N*ame of beggar / vagrant / waif:

*S*igned by workhouse keeper:

He wrote the date then turned to the beggar.

"Name?"

"I'm not telling you," the man said in a sulk. "And you can't make me."

"Give it here," Mrs Humble said. The policeman passed the notepad to her along with his pencil.

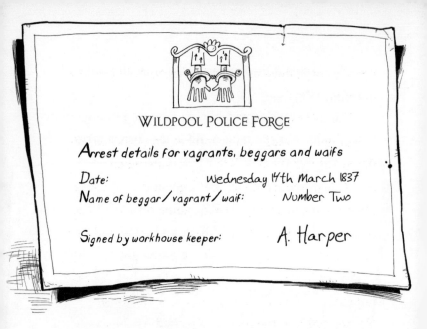

WILDPOOL POLICE FORCE

Arrest details for vagrants, beggars and waifs

Date: Wednesday 14th March 1837

Name of beggar / vagrant / waif: Number Two

Signed by workhouse keeper: A. Harper

She thrust it back at him and reached to close the door. "And don't show your ignorant faces here again till you have ninety-eight more."

She slammed the door.

Constable Larch looked at the form.

"Here, Liddle, that's a funny way to spell 'Humble'," he said.

"She's from the south," his partner explained.

"We'd better get off to Garth Court, I suppose."

Larch looked up at the darkening sky. "It'll be dark before we get there. It's dark enough in the daytime.

I'm not going there at night. It's scary. We'll go in the morning."

"Good idea, Larch."

Suddenly Liddle's hard top hat was knocked into the roadway. "What was that?" he squawked.

"Kids throwing stones. Let's get back to the High Street . . . the gas lamps will be going on soon." The two men shuffled as fast as their old legs would carry them, back over the bridge and into the town.

A man in an even more battered top hat stepped out from behind the corner of the workhouse. He stepped into the road and picked up the stone that had hit Liddle's hat. A scrap of paper was wrapped around the stone. He hurried back up the hill after the policemen. As they turned into the police station, he turned into Master Crook's Crime Academy.

The four students were sitting at their desks listening to Ruby Friday giving the latest lesson in kidnapping.

"How is Martin?" Nancy asked, anxious.

Mr Dreep unwrapped the paper.

COLD IN HERE. THE HUMBLES FEED ME COLD PORRIDGE WITH
MORE WATER THAN OATS. THEY HAVE A FIRE IN THEIR ROOM
BUT WON'T LET ME HAVE ONE. THEY WON'T EVEN LET ME
HAVE A CANDLE. I WILL BE FINE BECAUSE I'M ONLY HERE FOR
A DAY OR SO. DON'T WORRY, MILLIE.

MRS HUMBLE JUST TOOK IN A NEW INMATE. HE IS CALLED
TWO. BUT WE HEARD HER SAY THE MAYOR WANTS EVERYONE
FROM GARTH COURT IN HERE BY FRIDAY. AND FRIDAY IS THE
DAY OF THE VISIT.

LOVE MARTIN

Alice said, "So tomorrow we save the families in
Garth Court?"

"No, Master Crook didn't order us to save them,"
Mr Dreep said quietly.

"We'll see about that!" Alice said. She marched to
the wall and blew down a tube. A whistle sounded far
away in the basement. She placed the tube to her ear
and a voice said, "Master Crook here."

"I want a word with you," Alice said and slammed
the tube back in its place. Then she stamped out of
the door and through another door that led into the
basement. Smiff shook his head. "She never changes."

Mr Dreep looked at Ruby Friday. "So Friday is a
busy day at the workhouse, Miss Friday . . . is that the
day you'd choose for the kidnap?"

"Of course!" she said. "We have just been planning it."

A few minutes later Alice slipped back into the room and sat quietly at her desk. "So?" Smiff asked. "What did Master Crook say?"

The girl shook her head. "He said . . . he said we have to fight the battles we can win. There's no point fighting a battle you are going to lose."

Ruby Friday laughed. "The Duke of Wellington said the same . . . that's why he never lost!"

"But we're not going to war against the French," Smiff argued. "We're just going to stop two old policemen arresting a hundred poor people. Easy! We've beaten them before. We can do it again."

Samuel Dreep waved his fingers the way he did when he was excited. "Master Crook knows more than you think. If he says Garth Court is a battle we can't win then there is a reason. Something will happen there tomorrow that no one can stop."

"But we should *try*!" Nancy moaned. "Those poor families!"

"We can watch," Dreep said. "Watch and wait. Then make our plans."

"Remember Waterloo," Ruby Friday said. "Fight the battles you can win . . . and if you can't win . . . then cheat!"

Chapter 6

FEAR AND FIRE

Thursday 15th March 1837

If Wildpool workhouse was tombstone grey then Garth Court was as brown as the soil on a newly turned grave. Grime-brown brick walls round slime-brown earth floors and broken brown shattered doors and rough brown boards over brown holes that were once windows.

The people were brown. Brown rags on skin that was filth-brown and brown shadows round eyes that were empty as the windows. If you cut one in half you would probably find brown bones.

The walls rose three rooms high but there were crowded attics above them and a cellar where the cess

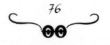

pit held the waste from the toilets. Four walls made a sunless courtyard in the middle where no weeds cared or dared to grow.

From the outside Garth Court looked like a deserted brown brick shell. From the inside it looked a lot like Hell.

The people of Garth Court were thin and hungry. Only the cats were fat from all the rats they caught. Garth Court was no place for rats. The children who caught them were as deadly as the cats and ten times as hungry.

Just a year before our story started, an inspector had gone inside the court. He came out without his jacket, wallet, hat or overcoat.

After four long weeks in hospital he found the strength to write one last report and then he took a job as a shepherd under the free, fresh stars. He said he'd never go near a town again. His report was hidden by Mayor Twistle, ashamed of such a sight that stood to blight his Wildpool Town.

Number 6 Garth Court. One large family shares a single room with two rabbits and songbirds in cages. The songbirds are kept for bird-singing competitions in the taverns.

Number 10 Garth Court. There is a trapdoor in the room linking it to a room above so a person can escape from one room to another when chased by the police.

Number 5 Garth Court. Two families share a room. The cupboard was used to keep the babies in.

Number 2 Garth Court. Eleven persons have been living in these two rooms for a long time. The rooms were in the most filthy conditions that can be imagined. There were four beds in the room with three persons to a bed. Behind the bed was a hen roost with a deposit of filth; the smell from the room was most overpowering.

And so it went on.

Sir Oswald and Lady Twistle made sure no one else saw that shameful report.

When Liddle and Larch had marched through the town towards Garth Court it seemed a hundred people had followed them. The two old men were in step, truncheons raised high.

They marched past Master Crook's Crime Academy and the teachers and pupils slipped out to follow them. "Today's school trip is probably going to take us to Garth Court," Mr Dreep said.

"Yes, well don't walk too fast cos my legs ain't as young as they used to be . . . and neither is me head, me teeth or me stockings," Ruby Friday huffed.

The constables marched through the flock of geese that were being driven to the butcher's yard. The angry, clacking geese turned and followed them. There was nothing the goose-girl could do to stop them. The constables walked around a small herd of cattle on their way to the market.

They marched THROUGH the geese but AROUND the cows. You can't march through a cow. It's like Ruby Friday said, "Only fight the battles you can win." So next time you see a cow in the road, walk around it. Next time you see a bull in the road just run. Unless you are a matador, of course.

The cattle turned and followed. They marched down Low Street and past Smiff's house.

Smiff's mum came to the door. "Hello, Smiff! You and that handsome Mr Dreep coming in for a cup of tea? I made it fresh yesterday."

"We're busy at the moment, Mum – I'll have it after school tonight," the rough-haired boy said. "I'll bring you some sugar!"

Mrs Smith smiled at her neighbour. "I'm so proud of our Smiff. You should see his school report! Bottom marks for honesty, bottom marks for helping the police and no marks at all for being polite to posh folk!"

"Takes after his mum, then," the neighbour muttered.

The constables were being followed by every stray dog in Wildpool and children were pouring out of the houses to join the stream down Low Street. "It's like a papered pie!" Mrs Smith chuckled.

80

"A what?"

"That story when we was kids. The children followed the Papered Pie and got lost in the mountains."

The neighbour frowned. "Don't you mean the Pied Piper?"

"That's what I said. Here! I'm getting my shawl. I'm not going to miss this!"

"But what's happening?" the neighbour asked.

"Haven't a clue," Mrs Smith shrugged, "but I don't want to miss out!"

It seemed as if half of Wildpool had gathered outside Garth Court. Mayor and Lady Twistle were already there, sitting silently in their carriage. The mayor stayed silent when the constables arrived. He simply raised a short arm and pointed a short finger at the entrance arch to the brown brick building.

Even the chattering children went quiet when Liddle and Larch marched in. For a minute you could have heard a rat squeak.

Well you couldn't have heard a rat squeak because most of the rats had been eaten by the cats. The rats that were left stayed alive because they had the sense to stay quiet. Let's say you could have heard a cat's footfall. That's foot-fall not foot-ball.

Smiff peered through the archway into the square courtyard. It was only a minute from his own home but it was very different. There was not a blade of grass in the square yard. He watched the policemen pick their way through piles of rubbish and broken furniture.

The windows were boarded but there were cracks in the boards and sly eyes seemed to follow the two men in navy uniforms. Someone had chalked words on a board beside a door-less entry:

It seemed like only a minute had passed before the two constables came back out blinking into the light. . .

Thursday 15 March 1837

THE WILDPOOL STAR
COPS IN COURT CATCH COLD!

Today Wildpool's new police force, Constables Liddle and Larch, were caught cold when they tried to enter Garth Court by the riverside. The shocked constables gave our reporter an interview as they stood shivering outside the brown buildings.

"We entered the premises as ordered. The windows were boarded up so we used our lanterns," said the ageing Constable Liddle. "The door closed behind me. First I felt the lantern snatched from my hand and shone in my face. That blinded me. I then felt things swarm over my body. They could have been rats or they could have been human hands!"

His terrified partner, Larch, added, "The same thing happened to me. I reached for my police rattle to call for assistance but it was gone. I reached into my pocket for my police notebook, but it was gone too ... I mean the pocket as well as the notebook. After a minute the swarming hands stopped, the door opened and I was thrown out of the door."

"Me too," Liddle said. "In the archway I bumped into a man. I reached for my truncheon to defend myself, but it had gone, along with the belt I hang it from. I was about to strike this man when I realized it was Constable Larch. I didn't

Cont.

recognize him because he was wearing only his underclothes – not even his boots. He looked embarrassed."

"And Liddle looked the same," Larch put in. "We were both stripped and thrown out within a minute. These people are expert thieves and it will take an army to get them out."

"The inspector said this was our chance to cover ourselves in glory," Liddle sniffled. "Now we're not covered in anything. Anything at all."

The brave constables posed while the Wildpool Star newspaper artist sketched them in their underwear. Ladies are asked not to look at this picture as they may be shocked.

A little child giggled but no one joined in.

"Is that why we're here?" Alice whispered to Mr Dreep. "To learn from expert crooks on how to outwit the police?"

The teacher shook his head. "No, Alice, these are not clever crooks, just desperate people. We steal from the rich to help the poor. But we never make the constables look foolish. That would be a big mistake. Mayor Twistle will just be angry."

"So? What can he *do*?" Alice asked.

Samuel Dreep just nodded towards the mayor's fine carriage.

Mayor Twistle's face hadn't changed. He stepped out of his carriage. He pointed up to the railway line that ran above the docks. Locomotive No. 3 stood at the end of the line. It was on a platform that ended high above the river. The coal trucks could drop their coal into the waiting ships.

The engine driver waved back. He tugged on the whistle of the steam train giving three long blasts. There were twenty trucks but not one lump or chip of coal inside. From each truck six men stood up. Even from far below the crowd could see they were large men with arms of solid muscle and faces hard as iron. They each carried a tool – pick-axes and shovels, metal levers and bow saws.

They formed up in a loose line – as loose as a line of ants but just as determined – and began to walk down the path towards the quayside.

"Ah," Mr Dreep sighed. "Navigators."

"What?" Smiff said.

"We call them navvies," Ruby Friday said. "They're the men that are building the railways. I guess these are the workers building the Wildpool and Helton line that'll join up with the Great Northern line."

"A dangerous job," Samuel Dreep breathed.

"Dangerous men."

The army of navvies didn't speak. When they reached Garth Court they split into two groups. Half formed a line like an iron wall outside the arch. The rest walked calmly through the archway into Garth Court. There was a splintering of wood.

There was no opening of doors that they could be locked behind, like the poor policemen. There were cries of frightened children, squeals of babies, quacks of ducks and screams of women.

I didn't mention the ducks before. It upsets me to think of the ducks. They are such comical and charming creatures. They lived in the room with one of the families. They were not pets. Their eggs were tasty. And when they stopped laying eggs . . . what can I say? Duck soup is also very tasty. As I say, it upsets me.

Soon after the last navvy had vanished into the last shattered doorway the brown-faced, frightened, shivering families began to stumble out.

The line of navvies in the roadway outside closed in so the Garth families were trapped. There was more splintering as the boards were hacked away from the windows to let in the light, let out the stench and uncover any dark hiding places.

When almost a hundred people were huddled into the ring of captors, one navvy, who seemed to be the leader, came to the door and nodded to the rest. They formed into a line two abreast with the families trapped between them and began to march up Low Street towards the High Street at the top.

They turned right on to the bridge and across it towards the workhouse at the far end.

The crowd who had come to see some sport had only seen half of it.

When I say "sport" it was no more "sport" than throwing Christians to the lions in ancient Rome. Sport is when it's a fair fight with rules. Sport is pelting your teacher with pellets dipped in ink and trying to get away with it . . . not that someone as sweet as you would ever dream of doing such a thing, would you?

Some of the navvies who had been inside came out and pushed the watchers back to safety.

Suddenly there was a crashing as the roof tiles exploded out. Pick-axes and crowbars appeared in the gaps and the rotting timbers started to tumble into the road below. When the roof had gone the navvies started to beat at the wooden walls. The worm-eaten timbers crumbled and showed the pitiful rooms that had once been home to a hundred humans. A few ragged blankets and clothes fluttered to the ground and the crowd covered their mouths to keep out the smell.

The mighty navvy arms worked as tirelessly as the pistons on Locomotive No. 3 and in half an hour Garth

Court was a tangled pile of timber.

The navvies left. The last one carried out two bundles of navy blue with silver buttons. He handed them to the two constables who scrambled into their uniforms.

At last Mayor Twistle allowed himself a smile. He reached into his pocket and pulled out a fat purse full of silver. He handed it to the head navvy. The man took it and tugged at the hair on the front of his forehead. He pointed to the pile. About five or six of his workers ran to the rubble with tinderboxes and set the filthy straw on fire. In minutes the timbers caught alight and the crowd had to step back and away from the furnace heat.

The mayor's horses snorted and reared in fear.

"Home James, and don't spare the horses!" Mayor Twistle cried and slid up the window.

The driver raised his whip. "He loves shouting that . . . even if me name is Jack."

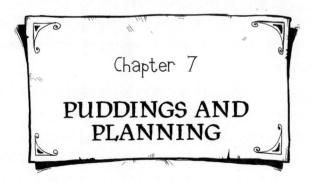

Chapter 7

PUDDINGS AND PLANNING

Thursday 15th March 1837

Alice White stood by the gates of the workhouse on the damp March day and watched the silent families troop in past Mr and Mrs Humble. The workhouse overseers rubbed their hands together and counted the pennies rolling through their doors.

It was noon and the previously fake but now real night soil men rumbled up to the gates. The taller night soil man grinned at Alice. "Thanks for speaking up for us in court," he said.

"It made all the difference," the smaller one agreed. "Anything we can do for you, miss, any time? A free load of night soil . . . it does wonders for your cabbages."

"I am *not* cooking cabbage in night soil!" the girl said with a shudder.

"Nah! You sprinkle it over your cabbage."

"I'd rather have salt and pepper," the girl said.

"I *mean* while the cabbage is still in the ground. The night soil helps them grow if you put it in the cabbage patch. When you pick your cabbage you'll be amazed!" the taller one said.

"I would," she nodded. "But I pick my cabbage from a shelf in the greengrocer shop."

"Oh, well, we can't do much for you then," the smaller man sighed.

"You're wrong!" Alice said quickly. "You *can* help me!"

And she told them how.

Millie Mixley climbed under the soil cart and clung to the axle. No one could see her unless they knelt down and peered *under* the cart. And *who* would do that?

I will bet Queen Victoria's purse full of pound notes that YOU have never crawled under a cart full of poo. Have you? See! I told you. If you want to sneak someone into a guarded place use a muck cart. I always thought it would be a good way to rob

a bank! I just never worked out why a muck cart would be driven through the bank doors. If you can think of something then do let me know.

When the cart was through the gates of the workhouse Millie dropped down. "Ten minutes today," the smaller night soil man said. "The place was nearly empty. Tomorrow it'll take twice as long now that all these people have arrived. Tell your brother to be here in ten minutes. We can't hang around."

The soil men started their round of the workhouse while Millie ran off to find her twin brother. She was in luck.

Martin was sitting at a desk just inside the door with a quill pen and a pot of ink, making a note of the new arrivals. They stopped and waited as dull as donkeys while he spoke with his sister. He quickly explained the job he was doing and showed Millie the sheet he was filling in.

Date	Name	Class	Age	No.
14 MAR 1837	MIXLEY, MARTIN	W	10	001
"	BEGGAR, BLIND	S	55	002
15 MAR 1837	JONES, JOHN	M	30	003
"	JONES, JANE	W	30	004
"	JONES, JOHN JUNIOR	W	10	005
"	JONES, JANE JUNIOR	W	6	006

"You just fill in the name and the class—"

"Class?"

"M for men, W for women and children, and S for sick and old – see? I'm a child!

"Write their number on a piece of paper and give it to them. Once they have had a bath they'll get a uniform. They have to pin this number on that. Then you pass them on to the beggar and he sends them off to different parts of the workhouse. The women and children under six go to one part of the building, the men to another, the children age seven to fourteen to another and the old and sick go to the hospital. It's easy."

"But what about if a man comes in with his family?" Millie asked.

"They're split up," Martin said.

"That's cruel."

"It's the workhouse rules," her brother nodded.

Millie looked at the list. "There's a lot of John Joneses," she said.

Martin shrugged. "When they don't want to give a name they just say John Jones. It doesn't matter anyway. Once they're in here they're just a number." He passed across a piece of paper with 001 written on it and pinned it to a uniform. "Here. Put this on and you are number one."

Millie took his place at the table. "The muck cart won't be long," she said. "Hurry. It's the only way out."

He nodded and ran out into the yard. Millie smiled up at the family that were waiting. They didn't smile back.

"Name, please?"

"Jones," the man said.

Outside the night soil men rolled into view. Mr and Mrs Humble were watching the new families arriving and didn't see Martin duck under the wagon and cling

to the axle. "Coming through!" the night soil men cried and the crowd shuffled aside to let the cart pass through the gate.

Constable Liddle and Constable Larch stood in front of Inspector Beadle's desk. They did not look happy.

"You entered Garth Court?"

"Yes, sir," lank Liddle muttered.

"And you let them strip you?"

"Yes, sir," large Larch sighed.

"How did Wildpool's wonderful police allow that to happen?"

Liddle and Larch looked at one another. "It was foggy, sir."

"Foggy!" Inspector Beadle roared.

"Yes, sir . . . they'd lit fires in some of the rooms. That made the damp walls steam, sir. It was a fog!"

This is a ridiculous excuse. People living in houses so damp they made a fog when they lit a fire. Ridiculous . . . but true. I was once so poor I lived in a house like that. It broke my nose. I ran to the door through the fog and missed . . . fog and mist? Get it? Oh, never mind.

"You have truncheons to deal with people who attack you. Did you use your truncheon, Liddle?"

"Yes, sir."

"And who did you hit?"

"Constable Larch, sir," the old man muttered into his moustache.

Larch nodded. "Made a right mess of my top hat, sir."

Inspector Beadle rubbed his eyes, eyes as small and dark as a pig's. "Get back on the streets. Our important visitor arrives at noon tomorrow. If anything goes wrong . . . anything . . . then I will use your truncheons to drive you over the edge of Wildpool bridge. Tomorrow is the most important day in Wildpool history. Nothing can go wrong. What can go wrong?"

"Nothing," the constables chimed together like the clock bell on Wildpool town hall.

The blind beggar showed a woman with her six children into a room like a cell. The walls were almost bare but there were straw mattresses on the floor and a bucket for a toilet in the corner.

On one wall was a finely stitched piece of cloth in a frame.

"IF ANYONE WOULD NOT WORK, HE SHOULD NOT EAT"

ST. PAUL

The woman (who called herself Mrs Jones) looked up and said, "Saint Paul? Is he the bloke that built the cathedral in London?"

"What cathedral?" the beggar asked.

"St Paul's Cathedral."

"Oh, yes . . . he's the same bloke. Very clever he is. Goes around stitching little mottoes for the poor . . . when he's not building cathedrals and things."

"If you don't work you don't eat, kids!" Mrs Jones said.

The six children nodded. "We *did* work, Ma," the oldest girl said. And it was true. Mrs Jones turned to the beggar.

"We worked ever so hard. We used to make matchboxes. If I made a hundred and forty-four then I got paid two pence. I picked up the cardboard and the sandpaper and made them . . . but we had to buy our own glue. Of course as the kids get older they can help. In the end we was making a shilling and sixpence a day. Two days' work and we paid the rent for the week. After three days we could afford to eat!"

The blind beggar nodded. "So what went wrong?"

Mrs Jones sighed. "Little Jacob got too hungry. One day he ate the glue."

"Ah," the beggar nodded. "Made from the bones of old horses. Glue is very tasty they tell me."

"Very tasty," little Jacob nodded. "When do we eat?"

"After you've had a bath and got into your uniforms."

The oldest girl looked at him. "What's a bath?"

Back at the academy, Martin Mixley stood in the front of the class. He felt a little strange. Not only were the pupils Smiff Smith, Alice White and Nancy Turnip looking at him. So were the teachers Samuel Dreep and Ruby Friday.

Miss Friday had already told them that the secret of a good kidnap is planning. "If we are going to make life better for the people in the workhouse we need to kidnap Mrs Humble. Show her the power the poor have if she doesn't mend her ways. But we can never be caught or it will be worse than ever. There are three rules that you must never forget – planning, planning and planning."

"You forgot to mention planning," Alice said sourly.

"First we need our kidnappers to know the plan of the workhouse, then we need to know where Mrs Humble will be at a certain time, and then we need to work on our disguises," Ruby Friday said firmly. "Now, Martin. The drawing of the workhouse!"

Martin pulled the sketch from inside his workhouse jacket and handed it to Samuel Dreep who pinned it to the blackboard. It was a very neat plan and even had some labels.

You may think Martin Mixley had a talent for drawing plans. You would be right. Many years later he became an architect and built some famous railway stations. He never did anything as great as St Paul's Cathedral . . . but, then, neither did Saint Paul.

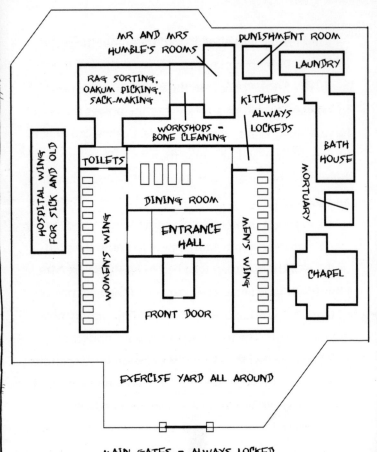

"Mr and Mrs Humble also have a timetable," Martin said.

"Oh! Wonderful," Ruby Friday cried and threw her hands in the air.

When they came down she tried to catch them but she couldn't because she'd thrown her hands in the air. Heh! Only joking. Let's face it . . . "throwing your hands in the air" is one of the silly things writers say when they don't quite mean it.

"Mrs Humble is asking to be kidnapped! Show us the plan."

FIVE A.M. Paupers rise and tidy their rooms, make the beds and wash the children while cooks prepare the gruel in the kitchen.

SIX A.M. Paupers gather in the dining room. They are served breakfast – one bowl of gruel each – and eat it in silence.

SEVEN A.M. Paupers go to workshops and begin work. Cooks prepare breakfast for Mr Humble. Bacon, eggs, sausage, lamb chops, kidneys, mushrooms, black pudding and fried bread with one pint of sweet tea and one pint of warm ale.

EIGHT A.M. Mr Humble arises, dresses, washes and has breakfast.

NINE A.M. Cooks prepare a light breakfast for Mrs Humble – the same as Mr Humble but with toasted bread instead of fried bread plus buttered crumpets, kippers and coffee.

TEN A.M. Mrs Humble arises, dresses and has breakfast.

ELEVEN A.M. Mrs and Mrs Humble do the accounts.

TWELVE NOON Mr and Mrs Humble meet at the front door to start a tour of the workshops, inspect the work, punish the slackers with beatings.

ONE P.M. If the work is good enough the paupers may be allowed to eat a lunch of soup and bread.

TWO P.M. Paupers return to work until seven p.m. Mrs and Mrs Humble have lunch together – roast meat, potatoes and carrots followed by suet pudding.

SIX P.M. Mr and Mrs Humble have supper of tea, pie, sandwiches, cakes, biscuits, sweetmeats, custard and tarts.

SEVEN P.M. Paupers have supper of cheese and broth.

EIGHT P.M. Families have one hour to meet while children play. Mr and Mrs Humble entertain guests to a late supper of cold meats, chutneys, cheese, biscuits, fine wines and brandy.

NINE P.M. Pauper prayers and return to cells. Lights out at 9:15 p.m.

"So, class?" Ruby Friday asked with raised eyebrows. "When do we snatch Mrs Humble, eh?"

It was Alice White who slowly raised her hand and said, "There's only one time, isn't there?"

Ruby Friday nodded.

Smiff sighed. "All right, miss clever drawers. When is it?"

Alice gave a smirk like a well-fed cat. "Work it out, pudding-brain. Work it out."

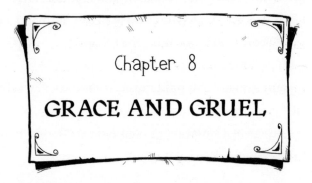

Chapter 8

GRACE AND GRUEL

Friday 16th March 1837

Mr and Mrs Humble were looking forward to the day . . . well, they couldn't look back because it was early morning.

Mrs Humble made a huge effort to get out of bed before six a.m. She even had her breakfast sent to her in bed so she could save time later. It was a large meal so it took her a long time to finish it but by half-past six she was dressing in her best blue gown.

"What time do our visitors arrive, my duckling?" she asked her husband.

"At noon, my sweetness. It all depends on the tide, of course, but I think Mayor Twistle meets her

at the south dock around now. He'll take her to his house in South Drive to rest from her journey. Then, at around half-past eleven, she'll ride here in the mayor's carriage in time to see the paupers working. By the time we've shown her around the building it will be time to watch the paupers eat."

"Then let's go down to the dining room and get them to practise," Mrs Humble said. "We don't want her to see them eating like termites at a timber-yard, do we?"

The couple linked arms and walked to the dining room where the paupers waited in silence for them to arrive. The cook had been told to serve no one till the Humbles arrived.

The families sat in rows on benches. Each had an empty bowl and a spoon. No one spoke. Even the babies were too weak to cry.

Mrs Humble smiled. "Today we will have a very important visitor. If you all behave well then you may get meat for supper tonight!"

"Then again, you may not," her husband muttered.

"There are ten rows of ten people. You are seated

there with number one at the front left and in order
up to number one hundred at the back right. First
numbers one to ten will line up and you will be given
a bowl of gruel," she said, pointing at the front row.
"You will return to your seats. But no one will eat till
all hundred have been served. You all eat at exactly the
same time. So much neater. Do you understand?"

Rows of dead eyes stared back at her.

"Excuse me, Mrs Humble!" the cook said. "I have
spent an hour cooking this muck."

"So?"

"So . . . you can't expect me to *serve* it as well. That's
not fair that's not. I am here as a cook, not a *server*.
They told me a pauper would do the serving."

*There's always one, isn't there? Someone who does
their job and nothing more? The teacher who says,
"Oh, I am paid to beat children till they learn – you
can't expect me to do yard duty." Or the cab driver
who says, "I am paid to take you to the station –
I'm not paid to carry your heavy bags to the train,
you old goat." But I'm here to tell you the story
of the Wildpool kidnap, not ramble on about lazy
teachers and cab drivers. So I'll get on with it.*

Mrs Humble sighed. "Very well, number one can help."

"Too small," the cook sniffed, looking down at Millie Mixley. "And dishonest too!"

"I'm not dishonest!" Millie cried angrily.

The cook waved a gooey ladle at her. "Yesterday you were wearing brown boots . . . today they are black. Paupers can't afford *two* pairs of boots . . . so you must have pinched them."

Millie's mouth moved like a goldfish. "Ah . . . ah . . . ah. . . I cleaned my brown boots with black polish by mistake!"

"I still don't trust you, boy. I don't want you helping me."

Mrs Humble ground her teeth. "Then number two can do it."

"I'm blind," the beggar said.

"So? That's no excuse." Her face began to turn red and angry. "Get yourself up on this platform and do as you are told otherwise you will be punished. You will spend a day in the solitary cell!" she raged. Then she lowered her voice. "There are no windows in the cell. Imagine that? Locked in darkness for a whole day."

"Ooooh! Sounds spooky!" the blind beggar gasped. "I'll serve the food."

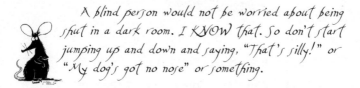

A blind person would not be worried about being shut in a dark room. I KNOW that. So don't start jumping up and down and saying, "That's silly!" or "My dog's got no nose" or something.

He stumbled on to the platform and picked up the ladle.

Mrs Humble clapped her chubby hands. "Numbers one to ten . . . except for number two . . . get ready . . . wait for it . . . and . . . *go!*"

The paupers, led by Millie Mixley at number one, lined up at the table where an iron pot full of gruel stood. The grey mush was slopped into their dishes and they returned to their seats.

The gruel was served out; the gruel disappeared.

"Now, we say thanks to our Lord. Our visitor will expect it!" Mr Humble said. Suddenly the paupers spoke. They spoke with one voice . . . but not the words Mr Humble expected. It was the pauper's grace.

THE PAUPER'S GRACE

The Pauper's Grace
"I thank the Lord for what I've had,
If I had more I should be glad,
But now the times they are so bad,
I must be glad for what I had."

"That's enough of that!" Humble growled. "Get on with it, Mrs Humble, before I lose my temper with these ungrateful wretches."

In Master Crook's Crime Academy the pupils ate fresh white bread with butter. They drank tea with sugar and sat by a coal fire to plan their day. Sausages sizzled in the pan and flames flared when the fat landed on the coals.

"It's noon, isn't it?" Smiff said. "You said there was only *one* time we could kidnap her. It's noon."

Alice smiled cruelly. "It took you all night to work it out."

"Alice!" Ruby Friday said sharply. "Do not bully your classmates. Remember the school rule?"

Alice scowled. "Sorry, Smiff. You are correct. The only time we can kidnap Mrs Humble is at *noon*. That is the time when the night soil cart enters the workhouse. It takes twenty minutes to make its round and at twenty-past twelve we leave with her."

"And at noon we know where Mrs Humble will be – in the entrance hall ready to start her rounds. We have Martin's timetable."

Ruby Friday nodded. "Two more things. We must

be sure we know which one is Mrs Humble."

"Easy," Martin Mixley said. "She's the stout one in the white dress with purple sleeves and a purple apron."

"I'll know her when I see her," Nancy said. "If she's stout even I will have trouble carrying her!"

"She will struggle. We need to get a gag in her mouth and a sack over her head in an instant," the teacher reminded them.

"And after Nancy has done that, I tie the sack up with rope," Alice said.

"And someone needs to get Mr Humble out of the way for a few minutes – we can't have him coming to rescue his wife."

"My job," Smiff said.

"That's it then. This morning in class we will work on our disguises," Miss Friday said. "There's nothing that can go wrong. Nothing that I can see."

The soot-stained water of the Wildpool river stood still when it reached the end of the pier. It mixed with the green water of the sea and pushed at it like a wrestler. The river lost the struggle in the end . . . as it did twice every day.

The tide flowed in and the fresh sea pushed back the filthy river where it came from; the dark river with its coal-dust and sewage, its drowned rats, its ooze and oil, its bits of boats and ropes and sawdust from the shipyards, a basket, a bucket and broken branches from far upriver.

The tide flowed in and brought with it a fine, large yacht with shining white sails that lit up the dull air. Sailors hurried over her decks, hauling on ropes, lowering the sails and steering her towards a rowing boat. A bare-footed sailor threw a rope to the rowing boat and let the oarsman tow them towards the quayside.

A man stood at the front of the yacht – the "prow" if you want the proper word.

He was an old man but as upright as the yacht's mast and with a face as cold as the water beneath them. His dark coat was cut from the finest cloth and his shirt from the best silk. But people noticed none of this.

People noticed, first, his hawk nose between his hawk eyes. They noticed his gleaming boots, tall, black boots that came up to his knees.

The yacht bumped gently into the quay. The tall

man walked to the door of the cabin and spoke quietly. "We are there, ma'am. We are at Wildpool."

The voice from inside snapped, "About time too. Even this bleak and black berth has to be better than another day at sea." Then the young woman's voice spat as if to a servant, "Dress me in my best purple dress. The one with the white collar, lace cuffs and hem. I suppose I will have to be polite to that awful little man. What's his name? Whistle?"

"Twistle, ma'am," the man on deck said. "Sir Oswald Twistle and Lady Arabella. He has a lot of power in this part of England."

"What do I care?" the voice called, muffled now as she wriggled into the too-tight dress. "Not as much power as I will have soon. So long as he feeds me well."

"Yes, ma'am. I'm sure he will."

"But I will have breakfast first . . . just to be on the safe side."

"Yes, ma'am."

At that moment the paupers in the workhouse put their spoons in their bowls and placed their bowls

on their knees to show they had finished their pitiful meals.

Suddenly Millie Mixley rose from her seat and walked to the overseer, basin and spoon in hand. She said – shocked at her own courage – "Please, sir, I want less."

Humble turned very pale. He gazed in amazement at the small rebel for some seconds, and then clung to the table for support.

Mrs Humble was weak with shock; the paupers with fear. "What?" said the overseer, in a faint voice.

"Please, sir," replied Millie, "I want less."

The master aimed a blow at Millie's head with the ladle. "Did you hear that, Mrs Humble? Pauper number one has asked for more!'

"For more?" said Mrs Humble. "Calm down, husband. Are you saying pauper number one has eaten his gruel and is greedy enough to ask for *more* than the amount we decided is good for him?"

"He did, Mrs Humble," replied the overseer.

"That boy will be hung," said his wife. "I know that boy will be hung."

No one argued.

Yes, I know, that the famed author, Charles Dickens, wrote a famous scene that very year of 1837, in which a boy called Oliver asked for more gruel in the workhouse. It is clearly nonsense. NO ONE who has tasted workhouse gruel would EVER ask for more. Not even the twisting little Oliver. THIS is the true story.

"Number two? Take him away to the punishment cell!" Humble ordered.

"If I can find it," the beggar said. "I'm blind, you know."

"Excuse me," Millie said in a piping voice growing stronger and angrier all the time. "But what is the charge?"

"Eh!" Humble exploded. "No *charge* . . . it's free, you foolish boy!"

"No, sir," Millie went on boldly. "I meant what crime are you *charging* me *with*? Remember Magna Carta?"

"Who's *she* when she's at home?" Humble sneered.

"An ancient law – no one can be arrested or locked away without being charged. It is my right as a freeborn girl. . ."

"Eh? You're a boy."

Millie looked down at her trousers. "Yes . . . my right as a freeborn *boy* . . . my right to British justice and a fair trial!" She raised a fist in the air.

Ninety-nine pauper mouths fell open. Then a bent old woman cried, "Well said, number one, lad!" and the room burst into applause.

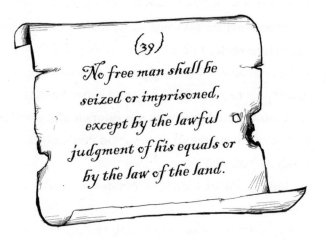

(39)

No free man shall be seized or imprisoned, except by the lawful judgment of his equals or by the law of the land.

Humble bumbled and searched for words. He read them off the motto on the wall, "If anyone would not work, he should not eat – that's what Saint Paul said."

The old woman rose to her feet. "We mostly *did* work till we were thrown out of Garth Court. I did dress-making."

"I was a weaver," a man's voice called. "Even if the

factories meant I didn't earn enough to feed a scarecrow."

"And I was a street-singer!" a young woman added. "I sang for pennies and I sang for my pride."

"I was an organ grinder . . . till those navvies wrecked my machine when they pulled down our home!"

The voices rose to a roar and Mr and Mrs Humble were white with fear. "Silence!" Mrs Humble screeched and the noise fell away. "We have a very important visitor this afternoon. If they think we are doing a good job then they will give us money . . . and the money will go to buy you better food, or finer clothes. You can work less hours and we'll even let you leave the workhouse to find better work. We promise that, don't we, Mr Humble?"

"We do. We promise!" he nodded.

Of course YOU know that as soon as the important visitor has gone he would break his promise. People who want something desperately enough will promise anything. "Ooooh! Mum! Buy me an ice cream and I will tidy my room." Yeah. Right.

The paupers nodded. Humble turned to Millie. "As for you, I will spare you the punishment room this time.

But no nonsense about asking for more at dinner time."

"*More?*" Millie frowned. "I asked for *less*! I couldn't *bear* to eat any more of that *slime*. I'd rather *starve*! But if you want me to ask for *less* when the visitor comes then I will, sir."

"No!" Mr Humble choked. "We want the visitor to think this is the best food a pauper has ever eaten!"

Millie nodded. "Right, so you want me to come and ask for *more*, do you?"

"Yes," the Humbles nodded.

"So the visitors think you starve us with too *little*."

Humble saw the trap too late. "No!" he moaned.

"So? What's it to be? 'Please, sir, I want some less' or 'Please, sir, I want some more'?"

The man's forehead was so creased his eyebrows touched his dark hair. His eyes looked as if they would explode. He had never had to think this hard in his life. "Say . . . say . . . 'Please, sir, I want some *more*'," he decided.

Millie grinned and looked at the paupers. "Great! Mr Humble said we could all have some more!"

In the rush to the front Mr Humble was trampled like a worm in a field of cows.

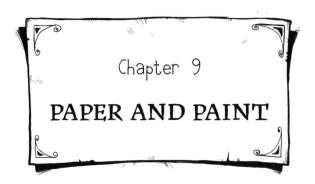

Chapter 9

PAPER AND PAINT

"The plan is in place," Ruby Friday said once the students of Master Crook's Crime Academy were back in the classroom. "Nancy Turnip, is the hiding place ready?"

Nancy smiled shyly. "The best place in the world, Miss Friday. The place where no one will ever look."

"Smiff, is the ransom note ready?"

"Yes, Miss Friday," he nodded and showed it to the class. It had a few blots and smudges but it was clear enough.

To Mayor Twistle,

We have Mrs Humble as a hostage.

She will live on gruel and water, just like the paupers, until you agree:

1. The paupers will be fed properly and that Police Inspector Beadle can check any time.

2. The paupers will be PAID for their work and the children will be free to play, not work.

3. The paupers will be free to leave the workhouse to find their own work any time they like.

4. The families will not be forced to live apart.

5. The paupers will be given proper clothes and not forced to wear uniforms and be ashamed.

If you do not agree in one day then Mr Humble will be kidnapped too.

We can kidnap anyone at any time. Guess who will be next, Mayor Twistle?

Pin your answers to the town hall door where all Wildpool can read them.

The Power to the Paupers Gang

PS Obey or else.

"Very good, Smiff. Now all we need to do is make the disguises. I have here some paper bags that you can carry in your pockets then slip over your heads when you need them," Ruby Friday said and handed one each to Smiff, Alice, Martin and Nancy. "Martin, you'll be staying here so as not to blow Millie's cover, but you can still learn this for next time. Now first cut out the eye holes, of course."

Smiff put the bag over his head and the eye holes were neat as a knight's helmet.

Alice pulled her bag over her head to try it. Smiff looked at her and gasped. "Oh, Alice! I have said some unkind things about you before."

"Uh?" she said, muffled under the bag.

"But can I say," Smiff said with a sob in his voice, "I have never seen you look so beautiful!"

There was a silence and Nancy and Martin looked at one another, waiting for the fight to start. Alice spoke sweetly. "Smiff?"

"Yes, lovely Alice?"

"What did I do before I came to Master Crook's Crime Academy?" she asked.

"You were a match girl, Alice."

"I was a match girl. And I still have my matches," she said quietly.

"Good for you, Alice," Smiff said.

"What would happen if I struck a match and set fire to your paper bag?" she asked.

Smiff slipped the bag off his head and placed it on the table. "Why not try it?" he asked with a grin.

At this point in the story I have to say, "Do not try this at home." If someone with a paper bag over their head annoys you it is WRONG to set fire to the bag. The whole house could burn down. And it's a waste of good paper.

Alice pulled off her paper bag. "I hate you Smiff," she said.

Smiff gasped. "Oh, Alice! Put the bag back on your head, *please*!"

The girl's fists went tight and Ruby Friday spoke quickly. "I think it would be a great idea to decorate the fronts of the bags to really confuse the police . . . just in case someone sees you and reports you!"

She took a paint-box from the cupboard and gave the students brushes and water.

Smiff painted a pair of spectacles and a dark moustache on a dark-haired gentleman – it could have been Mr Samuel Dreep. Alice painted a rough-haired boy that looked a little like Smiff. Nancy painted a cat's face and Martin painted a pig.

They had just finished and were washing their brushes when Mr Dreep swept into the room, his red-and-white striped scarf trailing like a sunset cloud and his top hat tilted back in the rush.

"Now, class, Mayor Twistle's guest has arrived

and she is being driven up to his house right now," he announced.

"A woman?" Smiff said.

"Who is it?" Alice asked.

Dreep shrugged. "I didn't recognize her but she must be a really important lady because she has an armed guard on the yacht – a tall old man was their commander and he has a troop of ten men in British army uniforms."

"Can we see them march past?" Martin asked, excited.

"They stayed on the yacht. Maybe they think the lady is safe in Mayor Twistle's care," the teacher shrugged.

Ruby Friday was pleased. "The mayor will be so busy with his guest it will make the kidnap of Mrs Humble all the easier."

"The soldiers and their commander are a worry," Samuel Dreep said.

Ruby Friday laughed. "I helped the Duke of Wellington win the battle of Waterloo. I know how to deal with soldiers, don't you worry!"

Constable Liddle and Constable Larch stood in front of the inspector's desk in the basement of the

police station on the High Street.

"You lost your trousers," the inspector said. *"The Wildpool Star* has told the whole town that the Wildpool police constables are clowns."

"We got our trousers back," Liddle muttered, "sir."

"No. Mayor Twistle's *navvies* got them back."

"We filled the workhouse," Larch pointed out.

"No, Mayor Twistle's *navvies* filled the workhouse. How many did *you* arrest?"

"Well," Liddle said eagerly, "there was that blind beggar!"

"And that chap on the corner of the High Street . . . the blind beggar!" Larch added.

"Er . . . did I mention the blind beggar?"

"Enough!" Inspector Beadle roared and he thumped the table with his massive fist. The police station shook. "Here is your chance to show the town . . . and a VIP—"

"What's a *vipp*?" Liddle asked.

"V.I.P. a Very Important Person," the inspector explained. "Mayor Twistle will be taking her around the town this afternoon. I want you on the streets."

"Sweeping them?"

"Yes. Keeping the roughs and scruffs off the street, making sure there are no traffic hold-ups, no dogs fighting, no stray animals. Here," he said, pushing a sheet of paper in front of them.

WILDPOOL POLICE FORCE
Orders for VIP Patrol.

Date: 16th March 1837

Polish your buttons and boots and brush your uniforms.

Proceed to the main streets of the town.

Patrol tirelessly. There must be NO farm animals being driven to market. NO stray cats or dogs. NO beggars or tramps.

Make sure every shopkeeper sweeps the pavement outside their shop.

Stop all vehicles if they are in the way of Mayor Twistle's carriage and the VIP.

If you are asked to walk in front of the carriage as a guard of honour then do it.

Then stand guard at the workhouse gates.

Wildpool needs you. Remember Mayor Twistle's words: "Carry your truncheons like flaming torches of justice. Bring light to the darkness of our savage streets."

Police Inspector Beadle

"Ooooh!" Constable Larch said. "It's a big job."

"But someone has to do it, and it is our proud duty," Liddle added with a sniffle.

"We are flaming torches!" Larch sobbed.

"No – you are flaming dribbling over my carpet," Beadle snapped. "Get out."

Mayor Twistle stood with his back to the fireplace. Lady Arabella sat on the sofa next to their VIP guest and looked up at her husband.

"I am proud to welcome you to Wildpool, ma'am," he said. "It's an honour."

"We know it is," the woman said sourly. She was short and stout with a pout to her snout that would have looked right on a pig. Talking of pigs, she was tucking into tea and scones with jam as her morning snack.

"When your dear uncle dies. . ."

"Won't be long now," the guest said and sucked thirstily on her tea.

"When he *does* die, then of course we will be proud to serve you . . . and maybe you will do us the honour of making our humble town into a city?" the little man said, twisting his hands.

"Maybe," the young lady said through a mouthful of scone. "Depends if we like the place. Doesn't look much."

"We are building warships for the navy – they will cruise the world, sail to every corner of the British Empire, and bring glory to the name of Wildpool City. . ."

"Town," she said.

It is sixty years on now. Wildpool never did become a city and I doubt it ever will. I think the old queen took a dislike to Wildpool. As for Mayor Twistle, he wanted to call himself LORD Mayor Twistle. A silly little thing I know . . . and maybe I am becoming spiteful in my old age . . . but I am very happy he never made it!

"Ah . . . yes . . . we built the best slave ships that crossed the oceans and made Britain rich."

The woman looked up sharply. "Slaving was banned three years ago," she said. "Go to America if you want to keep slaves these days."

"Ah . . . yes . . . but I meant—"

"And we do *not* mention the slave trade in London. It is not something we care to talk about," she said and rose to her feet. She was even shorter than the little mayor. "Now, we will rest," she said. "Then we'll get this over with."

Ruby Friday's plans were finished. Now she had to wait till noon. There was time for a walk in the dank March morning air to clear her head. There could not be any mistakes.

She walked along the High Street to the end of the bridge. Across the bridge stood the workhouse, closed and barred and almost silent. Only the odd chink of a hammer breaking rocks into smaller stones could be heard.

In the mist-muffled air, horses' hooves clacked softly on the cobbles and gulls cried sadly as they soared and dived round the fishing boats.

Below the bridge was the fine, large yacht Mr Dreep had described. Ten soldiers had lined up on the quayside and were practising their drill. They wore red coats and navy trousers with white cross-belts.

They carried long muskets with wicked knives on the end to stab and tear the guts from enemies who came too close.

The sergeant on the end lined them up in two rows

of five. The five at the front knelt down. They loaded their weapons faster than flying fish. They fired blanks towards the river and scared sixty seagulls into screeching flight. In moments the five in the back row had fired and by then the front row were ready to fire again.

They were good, Ruby knew. The very best the British army had. Ruby had mixed with soldiers all her life and had never seen better. Their faces were as hard as the concrete quay. What had the old Duke said in the Spanish wars about his own men? *"I don't know what effect these men will have on the enemy, but by God, they terrify me."* These were ten terrifying men.

Ruby Friday smiled. "They're the Duke of Wellington's own troop!" she laughed. She looked for their officer but he wasn't in sight.

There was an old gentleman stepping down from the yacht. He was not in uniform, yet he seemed to be in charge of the soldiers. His white hair and side whiskers curled out from under his hat. The troop stood to attention as he approached.

Ruby Friday strained her eyes. She rubbed them and looked again. But there was no mistake – even

from the bridge high above the quay she could see his large nose and those long black boots. "Holy crumpets," she breathed. "The Duke of Wellington himself! What's *he* doing in Wildpool? Holy, holy, crying crumpets!"

I am sorry if there are any younger readers or ladies reading this. I do not like repeating Ruby Friday's swearing. Polite writers, in the age of Victoria, would have written, "H—, H—, c— c—". But Victoria is dead . . . as I may have mentioned.

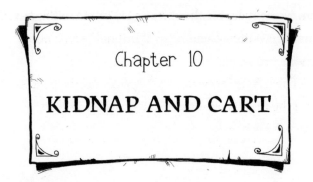

Chapter 10

KIDNAP AND CART

The new night soil men sat on their wagon at the end of the bridge. Alice gave them their last orders. They were about to set off for the workhouse at the far end of the bridge when they heard shouting.

"Move along there please! Get that wagon off the bridge!" Constable Liddle and Larch had turned from the High Street into Bridge Street and were using their truncheons to push people aside.

They sweated and panted up to the muck cart. "Get this to the side," Liddle cried. "Mayor Twistle's carriage is coming through. He doesn't want to be stuck behind a slow-moving vehicle."

Larch took the bridle of the horse in his hand and started to guide it towards the pavement then hurried on. No sooner was the cart at the kerb than the Twistle carriage clattered and rattled, rattered and clattled past.

The horses' hooves struck sparks off the cobbles and the mighty Wildpool bridge shook as they cantered across it.

There should be a law against driving too fast in town. It's even more dangerous now we have these smelly motor cars. The trouble is the really fast carriage and car drivers can't be caught by the police, can they? Well, not by police as old as Liddle and Larch. Maybe it's not such a good idea after all.

Dogs scattered and cats dodged. Liddle and Larch's boots sparked as much as the horses' hooves as they hurried to stand at the workhouse gateposts. They raised their truncheons in a salute.

The carriage skidded and bumped a little as it turned towards the Wildpool workhouse gates.

The sign usually said:

133

Now Mr Humble had been up a ladder with a pot of whitewash and added to it:

The gates swung open as the carriage arrived and swept in. The gates closed behind the carriage before Alice could see what happened next. And that's why the plan went wrong.

Mayor Twistle jumped down from the carriage and held the door open. He gave a nervous smile towards the Humbles. Mrs Humble was dressed in her best blue gown and matching bonnet and dropped into a low curtsey. Mr Humble pulled off his hat and bowed low.

The very important visitor in her purple dress stepped down, followed by Lady Twistle in pea-green silk.

"On behalf of a hundred happy paupers may we welcome you to Darlham Gaol," Mr Humble said.

"We're not there any more!" his wife hissed up at him.

"What?"

"We're not in jail."

"Oooops!" the workhouse overseer said and smiled. "We are not in a jail. We are in a happy place full of happy people who love their work."

"Oh, please!" the little visitor said with a wave of her tiny hand. "No speeches. Let's get on with it." And the mayor led the way to the main door of the building.

It was exactly noon. The town hall clock chimed, *ding-dong* and all that. But there was another *ting-tong* of a smaller bell.

"Excuse me!" Humble said. "There's someone ringing the bell at the gate! Probably the muck men!"

He shuffled across to the gate and lifted the bar.

Alice had run across to the workhouse gate but it had slammed in her face. "Holy crumpets," she snarled.

This is what Ruby Friday used to say. It just goes to show that adults can give young people disgusting habits like swearing. Do NOT do it, adults. And, young readers. Do NOT let me hear you repeat this disgraceful language either. Sadly I have a duty to report what was said. That does NOT mean you should copy.

She ran back to the cart. The girl lifted a canvas cover that had been thrown over the back. The cart had been scrubbed clean . . . though it still smelled slightly worse than a coal-miner's armpit. Smiff and Nancy jumped down, climbed under the wagon and clung to the axle.

Alice pulled her paper bag over her head then nodded to the night soil men. They tapped the horse and guided it towards the gate.

"Halt! Who goes there?" the constables said.

Later, when the "Wanted" poster was put up around the town, they remembered that face. . .

WANTED

MYSTERY BOY

WANTED FOR KIDNAP

SQUARE SORT OF HEAD, DARK HAIR, BLUE EYES,
LARGE MOUTH, SKIRT (TO TRY AND FOOL YOU
INTO THINKING HE'S A GIRL), BROWN BOOTS,
BROWN SKIN.

REWARD OFFERED FOR HIS CAPTURE
DEAD OR ALIVE
10 GUINEAS

Alice peered through the holes in her mask. "You can see who it is. It's the new night soil men – the ones you arrested. This is their punishment . . . emptying the workhouse toilets for a week."

"So it is, little boy," Larch said and patted Alice on the head. He frowned. There was something not quite right.

Larch reached across and pulled the bell. The town hall clock was giving its twelfth *dong* when the gates swung open and Humble's flat face appeared.

"What do you want?" he demanded.

"Night soil men!" Larch cried. "It's all safe. We checked."

The overseer scowled till his thick eyebrows almost knitted themselves into a scarf over his nose. "We have a guest today. We have to be extra careful."

"We checked—" Liddle began.

"Checked? Did you check under the canvas cover? There could be a small army of assassins hiding there!" Humble cried.

"Well, they wouldn't be hiding in a pile of poo, would they?" Larch argued.

"And it's not our job to poke our noses into night soil," Liddle grumbled.

138

Humble stumped to the back of the cart and raised the canvas. "Hah! See?"

"See!" Liddle cried. "An army of assassins! Ooooh! I'll just run and get help."

"Stay there you cowardly cop. I mean, see, the wagon is clean and empty."

"So it is! That's all right then." Larch waved up to the drivers. "Carry on."

"Back in twenty minutes," the smaller night soil man said and whipped the horse into life.

The policemen took up their positions at the gateposts again. "It would take a cunning assassin to get past us," Larch chuckled.

"Would it?" Liddle asked.

"Well . . . yes. Liddle and Larch are too clever to be caught out," Larch said. The constables shuffled their cold feet on the pavement. Their eyes were just a little uneasy behind the smiles.

"Oh, yes. Much too clever."

The wind off the river whipped at Liddle's flowing white moustache and they stood there for a silent minute. Finally Larch said, "That boy."

"Yes."

"When I patted him on the head. . ."

"Yes?"

"I thought I heard him . . . rustle."

"Me too."

"Very odd."

Alice stood at the south-west corner of the workhouse
and watched the muck cart finish its round and roll
towards her. She sped to the south-east corner, paper
bag flapping in the wind, and waved at Smiff. The boy
in the gentleman-faced mask ran in through the front
door. The group of visitors stood in the entrance hall
admiring the painting of Mayor Twistle that hung on
the wall, grinning like the skull on a pirate flag.

"Fire!" Smiff cried. "Hurry, Mr Humble. There's a
fire in the punishment room!"

The overseer dashed through the dining hall, past
rows of astonished paupers waiting to start their meal,
and into the dark cell.

"Fire? Where?" Humble grumbled.

"There!" Smiff pointed. "In that room!" As Humble
leaned forward to look, Smiff pushed him inside and
swung the door shut.

Mr Humble may have cried, "Help! Let me out!" But, if he did, no one heard a thing because the walls were as thick as a Wildpool policeman's head and the door as solid as their truncheons.

Smiff raced back through the dining hall, giving Millie a small wave as he ran past her. The Twistles, Mrs Humble and their guest were standing looking alarmed. "Mr Humble is dealing with it," he said quickly. "He says he wants you all to go into the dining hall. Dinner is served. Step this way!"

As the visitors moved towards the dining room door Smiff raised a hand and pointed. "That's her, Nancy . . . the one in the purple dress."

Nancy, in her mask of a cat, paused a moment . . . *"She's the stout one in the white dress with purple sleeves and a purple apron."* That's how Martin had described Mrs Humble. This woman was stout all right, but the dress was purple with white, not white with purple. Nancy gave a tiny sigh – boys had no interest in women's clothes. Martin had got it *wrong*.

Neither Smiff or Nancy noticed Mrs Humble in the blue dress, who had opened the door to the dining room to welcome the visitors.

"After you," Mayor Twistle said to their guest.

"No!" Smiff hissed to him. "The room is a mess! You and Lady Twistle go and sort it out."

The mayor gave a terrified grin. "Excuse us . . . we . . . the mayoress and I . . . we just need to make sure everything is in order." Oswald Twistle pushed his wife ahead of him and closed the door.

The visitor blinked. Smiff smiled at her. "Here is a poem I wrote for you," he said. He stood with his back to the door as Nancy crept behind the guest. The boy chanted:

"Roses are red, pink, white and fancy.

Now it is time for the kidnap, dear Nancy!"

Nancy threw a sack from the sheep-head shop over the woman's head and clamped a hand over her mouth so she couldn't scream. The woman struggled and Nancy stumbled as she pulled her victim towards the door.

Using all of her strength, she lifted the chubby woman off the floor and carried her out of the door before the other visitors could come to find out what was happening.

Alice was waiting with a rope and tied it firmly

round the sack so the woman's arms were tight against her sides and the sack held firm. The muck cart came around the corner at exactly the right moment and the victim was thrown on to the back.

Yes, clever reader, you remembered that NOW the cart was NOT empty but full of workhouse waste. This was sad but it couldn't be helped.

The canvas cover was placed over the top and Smiff ran to open the gate before climbing under the wagon with Nancy.

The policemen raised their truncheons in salute then realized it was the muck cart, not the mayor's carriage.

"Want to search the back again?" Alice asked through her mask.

Constable Larch's large nose twitched at the smell from the cart. "I don't think so," he said. "Not unless you are stealing night soil again!"

Alice laughed. "No, Constable. We have something much more disgusting on board!"

"Ho! Ho!" the policemen chuckled. "Off you go!"

Alice led the horse on to the bridge and turned into

the High Street. Shoppers turned away and covered their noses as the cart creaked past. At Master Crook's Crime Academy, Smiff and Nancy dropped off the axle.

The boy ran into the school but Nancy climbed up alongside the night soil men. She whispered orders to the drivers.

"Where are you taking her?" Alice asked.

Nancy shook her head. "Secret, Alice. It's what Ruby Friday said. The less people know, the better."

Alice looked furious even through the paper bag. "You don't trust me!"

"Of course I do . . . but, if you don't know where I'm going, you can't betray me. If the police tortured you then you might tell. You'd hate that, Alice."

The paper bag with the boy's face nodded and Alice turned to follow Smiff into the school.

The muck cart moved on.

To where? I can't tell you. But it was just as Nancy promised. "The best place in the world, Miss Friday," she had said. "The place where no one will ever look."

144

Alice and Smiff tore off their masks and ran into the classroom. Mr Dreep and Martin waited for them.

"Well?" Dreep asked.

"Perfect," Alice cried. "Just perfect."

The constables stood at the gate and the wind off the sea blew it open.

"Hello!" Liddle said. "No one locked it behind the muck men. We don't want the paupers escaping. We'd better go in and bar it."

They stepped through into the courtyard.

From inside the workhouse came a roar like a train getting closer. It had started when Mayor Twistle had walked into the dining room. Now it was so loud it could be heard outside.

Millie had stood up to say to Mayor Twistle, "Please, sir, I want some more". The plan was that the rest of the paupers would join in and cause such a disturbance no one would notice Mrs Humble was missing . . . or at least not until the muck cart was well away.

Millie had jumped to her feet and said, "Please, sir, I want some . . . what's Mrs Humble doing here?"

145

"Eh?" Mayor Twistle said. He looked at the overseer's wife in her best blue dress and matching bonnet. "She works here, foolish boy."

"Yes, I know, but she was supposed to have been—" Millie started to speak but the blind beggar cut in.

"The lad was just about to ask for more!"

"Yes!" the paupers cheered. "We want more! We want more!"

Soon they were roaring their chant. The constables were hit by the wave of sound as they stepped into the dining hall.

"Is everything all right?" Larch asked the mayor.

"Just a stupid little riot about food."

"No," Liddle shouted so he could be heard. "We meant, is everything all right with the VIP?"

Mayor Twistle looked around. His eyes widened, his mouth worked but no words came out. He ran to the door and looked into the entrance hall. Only his own face on the portrait looked back.

He rushed into the courtyard where his driver dozed on the carriage seat.

"James! Have you seen our guest?"

"No, sir . . . and me name's Jack."

146

Sir Oswald Twistle dashed back into the room where the chanting had fallen silent. "Arabella," he asked, "where is our guest?"

"In the hall? Back in the carriage?"

"No, she's not," the mayor said in a voice like a frog with a sore throat.

But Lady Twistle's voice was strong. "Kidnapped!" she wailed.

Frantic, the mayor grabbed Constable Liddle by the front of his jacket. "Call the police!"

"We ARE the police."

"There has been a kidnapping!" he said, shaking him till his buttons rattled.

Millie was paler than the gruel. She looked at Mrs Humble – the woman they were meant to snatch – she looked at the trembling mayor. "But *who* has been kidnapped?" she muttered.

Chapter 11

SEARCHING AND SHOOTING

Go out on a moonless night and shine a lamp in a field of rabbits. Catch the eyes of a rabbit. The rabbit will be frozen with fear, unable to move. That makes it easy to shoot.

This trick, called "lamping", is used by poachers. This is one of the many useful tips you will pick up by reading my Master Crook chronicles. I ask for no further payment . . . just send me a tasty piece of rabbit pie.

That is how Mayor Oswald Twistle looked that day. His wife took command. "We must tell the Duke of

Wellington at once," she said.

"He'll have me shot!" Sir Oswald sobbed.

"Probably," she agreed. "But if you *don't* tell him he'll find out sooner or later and he'll have you even *more* shot. It is *his* job to guard the lady. He thought she'd be safe in the hands of a mayor – he didn't realize how careless you could be, Oswald. But never mind. The Duke beat Napoleon – a gang of kidnappers will be no problem."

Mayor Twistle nodded and walked stiffly to his carriage. Constables Liddle and Larch wandered after him. "You two climb on the back," Lady Arabella ordered. Then she called to the coach driver, "Drive to the quayside, Jack, and drive as if your life depended on it!"

Jack cracked the whip and the horses trotted towards the workhouse gate. The paupers watched in wonder as the carriage skidded through the gates that the policemen had left open.

It bounced over cobbles and threatened to squash rats and cats flat. The constables were flung from side to side and their boots bounced up and down on the platform at the back. "I feel sick," Liddle moaned just as the carriage left the ground and crashed back down

to send his stomach into his mouth.

The carriage reached the quayside and shot past boatyards and barns and barges and ballast and bollards with ropes wrapped round, past fish filleters, carpenters, captains and coal carters, riveters and riggers, boiler builders, smiths and sail stitchers, sailors and tailors, craftsmen and draughtsmen, mastmakers and mates, chandlers and horse handlers, clerks on barques, seamen on steamers, workers on wherries and fat men on ferries.

The soldiers were cleaning their weapons on the deck of the yacht. They jumped to their feet when they saw the careering carriage come to a halt. They lined up quickly as a guard of honour for their guest.

The Duke of Wellington came out from his cabin and pushed through them to see Sir Oswald Twistle tumble from the carriage. The Duke put on his hat and waited. "Oh, your Dukeship!" the little man wailed. "We have lost her!"

The Iron Duke's iron face hardly moved. "Lost?"

"We think she's been kidnapped," the mayor moaned.

"Tell me," the Duke ordered.

Sir Oswald's tale poured out. It was a jumble of

words about paupers and gruel but at last the Duke
began to make sense of it. "I left her in your care,
Mayor," he said.

"Are you going to shoot me?" Twistle whispered.

"God's teeth no, man! We need your help to find
her! You are no use to me *dead*! No. We will find her
first . . . and *then* I'll think about shooting you."

"Thank you, sir," Oswald Twistle said with a weak
smile.

The Duke of Wellington lined up the troops and
the policemen on the quayside. He spoke quickly. "We
came to Wildpool with an important visitor. We kept
her name a secret because we feared she would be
kidnapped. We left the soldiers on the yacht – we didn't
give her a full army escort because we didn't want
people to suspect she was *really* important. But she is.
She is the most important woman in Britain and we
have to find her. She is Princess Victoria. And, when the
old king dies she will become Queen Victoria."

"Do you know who we are?" Princess Victoria said.
She was bound to a chair and looked up at the cat-
faced mask of Nancy.

"Yes," Nancy nodded. "You are Mrs Amelia Humble of Wildpool's Wonderful Workhouse."

The princess twisted her smooth, round face in scorn. "We are NOT."

Nancy sighed. "All right. You are Mrs Angela Harper of Darlham Gaol."

"We are most certainly *not* from a gaol. How dare you!"

Nancy shook her head. "It doesn't really matter what you call yourself today, the fact is you are our prisoner and you will sign this ransom note." Nancy thrust the note in front of the young woman's face.

My Dearest Hengist

They have imprisoned me in a secret hideout where no one will find me. Someone will deliver a note to you and Mayor Twistle soon. They will ask for the paupers to be well fed and clothed. Sign that note and I will be set free. Refuse and they say they will cook me in a large pot and feed me to the paupers. Please, my sweetness, do as they say.

Signed:

The princess glared at Nancy's cat face. "Do we *look* like a workhouse keeper?"

"Don't know. I never met Mrs Humble."

"Look at the ring on our finger . . . it is a ring of state. We are going to tell you who we are. You are then going to set us free. If you *do* then you will go to prison for fifty years for treason. If you do *not* then the Duke of Wellington will find us. He will arrest you and shoot you. Do you understand?"

Nancy nodded. "I'll tell you what. I will go and talk to Miss . . . our leader . . . and see what she says." She turned to go.

"Wait!" Princess Victoria cried.

Nancy stopped.

"Get us a fresh set of clothes and a warm scented bath. We have been carried in some sort of muck cart! We! Princess Victoria. Future Queen of Britain! At least let us get rid of this disgusting stench."

Nancy nodded. "I will get the servants to set up a bath, towels and clean clothes through that door in the dressing room. When they have done it they will knock on the door. You will count to ten then enter and have your bath. The rooms will be locked on the

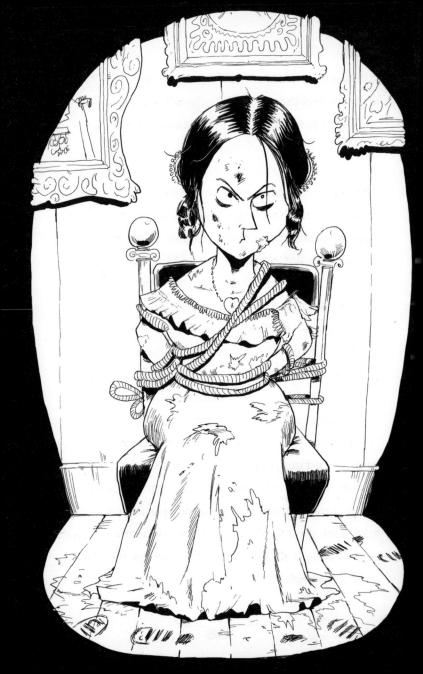

outside. You can't get out. But you mustn't see the servants and they mustn't see you. Understand?"

The princess glowered. "We understand. Now untie us."

The Duke of Wellington leaned close to Mayor Twistle and breathed in his face. "I have heard stories about your work in Garth Court," he said, waving a hand towards the flat, bare patch of earth where the houses had stood. "You can command a hundred thuggish railway workers."

"Yes, Duke Wellington, sir," the mayor said, swallowing fear like it was a bumble bee.

"There are . . . what . . . two thousand houses in Wildpool?"

"Yes, Duke Wellington, sir."

"I want those hundred navvies to search every one. Every room, every attic, every cellar. It's only twenty houses each. They will kick down locked doors if they have to. They will be split into groups of ten – each group will be under the command of one of my soldiers. If anyone gets in the way my men have orders to shoot."

"Yes, Duke Wellington, sir."

The Duke pointed to Constable Liddle. "Run up the hill to the coal platform. There's a train unloading now. Take it to the end of the line and collect the navvies. Bring them back here. Well? What are you waiting for?"

"Do you know how old I am? I can't run," Liddle groaned and sucked on one end of his white moustache.

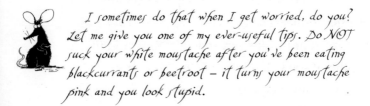

I sometimes do that when I get worried, do you? Let me give you one of my ever-useful tips. Do NOT suck your white moustache after you've been eating blackcurrants or beetroot – it turns your moustache pink and you look stupid.

The Duke drew a pistol. "I can shoot. If you are not at the end of the quay by the time I count to ten then I will shoot you."

Liddle found he could run after all.

The Iron Duke turned to Larch. "Run to the harbour-master's office. No vessel of any kind may leave the harbour until the princess is found."

Larch waddled away in a sort of run.

"How many roads are there out of Wildpool?"

"Just the Great North Road – north and south, Duke Wellington," the mayor squeaked.

"Get your driver to drop you off at the southern end of town and stop all traffic . . . he can then drop your wife at the northern end to stop our kidnappers escaping that way."

Mayor Twistle bounced down the gangplanks of the yacht to obey.

The Duke of Wellington turned to his troop. "Collect bullets and powder from the locker and be sure your muskets are loaded. We would like to capture these kidnappers alive . . . but, if they die escaping, it's their bad luck." The rock-faced men moved quietly and quickly. The Iron Duke had fire in his iron eyes as if he were almost enjoying being back in action. "These kidnappers are good – but the world's best kidnapper is not as good as me. Hah! Not even Ruby Friday could beat me. I wonder what ever happened to old Ruby?"

Ruby Friday sat in the classroom of Master Crook's Crime Academy. The pupils looked at her and waited.

"So, Smiff, you never got to give the ransom note to Mayor Twistle?"

"Sorry, I waited at the corner of the High Street – the way we said. The carriage would slow down as it turned to the police station. That's what you said."

"So what went wrong?"

"It didn't go to the police station. It raced down to the quayside and along to the fine yacht that sailed in this morning," Smiff told her. "The mayor seemed to be talking to an old man on the deck then he raced off towards the Great North Road."

"Please, miss," Martin asked quietly. "What's going on? Millie's still trapped inside the workhouse. What will I tell our mum? If she doesn't come home?"

Samuel Dreep's fingers had been whirring like someone with invisible knitting. "Millie is safe enough in there for the moment. We need to work out why the kidnap of Mrs Humble caused such a panic. She's only the wife of a workhouse overseer."

"Because we didn't kidnap Mrs Humble," Nancy said, walking in the door. She had taken off her cat mask and her face was pale and frowning. "The

woman I kidnapped is saying she is Princess Victoria. I think I grabbed the wrong person."

Ruby Friday frowned. "I should have guessed. *That's* why she has an armed guard led by the Duke of Wellington himself. Is she safely hidden?"

"Yes," Nancy nodded. "You told me to keep it secret."

"Better whisper it to me," Ruby Friday said.

As she spoke Ruby's round, rosy face split into a wide smile. "Oh, that is very good, Nancy . . . brilliant."

"But I'll have to let her go. We've failed, haven't we?"

Ruby shook her head. "Not yet, my girl. The best crooks can change their plans when things go a little wrong. Isn't that right, Mr Dreep?"

The teacher said, "It is."

"So, Smiff, get ready to write us a new kidnap note!"

Smiff lifted the lid of his desk and took out a fresh sheet of paper and a quill pen. He began writing.

Dear Mayor Twistle,

We have **Princess Victoria** as a hostage. Not even the Duke of Wellington will find where we have hidden her. Not unless we tell him.

She will live on gruel and water, just like the paupers, until you agree:

1. The wicked Mr and Mrs Humble will be sacked.
2. A pleasant lady called Friday will come to you tomorrow. You will give her the job as overseer.
3. She will change the rules so the paupers are free to come and go as they wish and families will not be forced to live apart
4. The town council will build a new, clean Garth Court with proper windows, wide chimneys, good toilets and made of the finest brick and plaster. When it is finished the workhouse families will be able to rent rooms for just one shilling a week.

If you do not agree in one day then we will tell the Duke that **YOU** have kidnapped the Princess Victoria. He will shoot you.

Sign below to show you agree to our demands

The Power to the Paupers Gang
signed:

"What can *I* do?" Alice cried. "This is the most exciting thing we've ever done in class and I've just been a lookout and not much else."

Mr Dreep looked worried. "We could give you the job of delivering the note to Mayor Twistle but—"

"I'll do it!"

"But it could be very dangerous."

"Who says? You says?" Alice jeered. "Danger is my middle name."

"I thought that 'stupid' was your middle name," Smiff muttered.

"He headed off to the Great North Road, isn't that right, Smiff?" Alice asked.

"Probably to stop the kidnappers escaping," Samuel Dreep put in. "That's what I'd do."

"I'll find him," Alice said.

"You'll need your mask!" Dreep warned.

Ruby Friday scribbled a note in pencil and put it in an envelope. She dripped sealing wax on to the flap and shut it. "If Mayor Twistle refuses then give him this."

Alice snatched up both letters and ran off . . . just in time. Mr Dreep locked the front door behind her. He returned to the classroom.

"What next, Miss Friday?" Martin asked.

But a hammering at the front door answered him. "Open up."

Mr Dreep left the classroom, walked down the corridor and unlocked the front door. A large man with skin as grimy as his work-clothes stood there. "I've come to search your house," he said.

"Have you a search warrant?"

The man let a slow smile spread across his face. "Yes."

"Can I see it?"

The navvy put three fingers in his mouth, turned and whistled. A soldier in a red jacket appeared in the gateway and raised his musket. It was aimed at a spot between Mr Dreep's eyes.

"Hmm," the teacher said. "That search warrant seems to be in order . . . come in. Could I offer you a cup of tea?"

While the navvy started in the attic rooms of the Crime Academy, and barged through doors, Ruby Friday slipped out of the kitchen door. She climbed the fence into the police station garden next door and came out

into the High Street from the police station gate.

The world's greatest kidnapper hurried along the High Street, past screaming children, sobbing women and cringing men. The people of Wildpool were gathering in the street as the army and the navvies stamped and stomped and stormed through their homes, shops, sheds and cellars.

Inspector Beadle stood at the door to the police station. "What are they *looking* for?" a woman cried.

"It's a secret," the inspector said. "A secret you may never know."

But still they didn't find the princess.

Chapter 12

BACON AND X

When Mrs Humble opened the door to the punishment room Mr Humble's face was white.

By the time he had marched to the dining room it was purple with rage. The paupers cheered him.

"What?" he roared.

"We want more!" they cried.

"More? More! You aren't getting *any*." He held up the key. "Some jester locked me in the punishment room. Our important guests went away in some sort of panic. You will *all* pay for that. The gates are locked. No one can escape. The kitchen is locked. No one can eat . . . not so much as a spoonful of gruel. The men will break one

ton of stone till their arms and backs ache. The women will pick ten sacks of oakum till their fingers bleed. The children will pick the seeds from ten sacks of cotton – and if there is one seed in the ten sacks they will be beaten by Mrs Humble's rods, won't they, Mrs Humble?"

"I'll enjoy it," the woman said.

"The sooner you start the sooner you will eat . . . probably tomorrow afternoon," he said.

The starving paupers, defeated, trooped away to their tasks.

Mayor Twistle stood in the chill east wind and argued. A queue of carts and horses were getting angry. "No one may pass!" the little man cried.

"Why not?" a farmer in a filthy smock asked.

"Because the Duke of Wellington says so," the mayor argued.

"The Duke of *Wellington*? Old Welly himself in Wildpool? If Welly's in Wildpool I'll eat my wellington boots!" the filthy farmer jeered.

The horse began to plod forward. "Fine!" Oswald Twistle said. "So long as you let me look in the back of your carts I can let you go!"

"What you looking for?"

"It's a secret."

"I haven't any of those on board," the farmer laughed. "Just a few geese. Mind they don't bite you."

Mayor Twistle raised the canvas cover. A goose bit him on the nose.

After twenty carts had been searched Mayor Twistle was almost pleased to see a boy with scruffy hair and a black skirt on run up to him waving an envelope. "Message for you, Mayor Twistle," Alice said.

"Oh," he moaned, stamping his frozen feet. "I hope it's from the Duke telling me I can come back to town!"

He tore open Smiff's ransom note and read it. He began to choke as if someone was pulling his necktie tighter than a hangman's noose.

The mayor looked at Alice's painted mask. "This is nonsense. You can't expect me to give in to these . . . threats!"

"You refuse to sign?" Alice sighed.

"Of course I refuse, you stupid little man!"

"Then you'll be shot . . . you stupid little man!" Alice said and thrust Ruby Friday's letter into his hand.

The mayor tore open the seal and unfolded the letter. He wobbled. He swayed. He staggered a few paces. He dropped the letter. He sobbed.

Alice picked up the letter and peered at it through the eye holes in her mask.

Mayor,

Princess Victoria is a prisoner in YOUR house. See if you can explain THAT before the Duke shoots you. Sign our note or we will tell him WHERE to find the princess and that YOU are the kidnapper.

A Friend

"Ohhhh!" the mayor groaned. "I'm too young to die. What am I to do?"

Alice pulled a pencil from her pocket. "Sign the paper, of course," she said.

Mayor Twistle signed.

*

The grey-faced, grey-haired butler stood at the door to 13 South Drive – Mayor Twistle's home. He wore a black tail coat, grey trousers, white shirt and white cravat tie. "You rang?"

The navvy was broad as the door and carried the handle from a pick-axe in his hard hand. "I've come to search the house," the man said.

"Certainly, sir. Just show me your search warrant and I will be happy to show you round."

The man raised his pick-axe handle and pushed it under the butler's nose. "Here's my search warrant," he said, as he'd said at the other houses.

"Ah!" the butler smiled. "I can tell you have been sent by Mayor Twistle!"

"That's right."

"Then you will be delighted to know *this* is Mayor Twistle's house."

"So?"

"So-o-o, Sir Oswald would not send you to search his own house, would he?"

"No, but. . ."

"In fact he may be just a touch upset if you trampled your muddy boots over the carpet that the

168

maid has just swept," the butler said quietly. "What is your name?"

"Me name? I don't have to give me name!" the navvy said in alarm.

"The mayor will be so pleased with your work. When it comes to rewards your name will be top of the list!"

"Well," the navvy said, "when I sign for my pay I usually mark it with a 'x'."

The butler passed him a scrap of paper and a pencil. "Just write it down here."

The man did as he was asked.

"Thank you!" the butler said. "I will see this is delivered to the mayor, in person, when he gets home. I will tell him what a fine man you are and the reward will be doubled."

"Thanks mate," the navvy said.

"Good night and good luck!" the butler said as he closed the door.

A girl stood behind the butler. She wore a paper mask with the face of a cat on it. "There you are, Nancy, you're safe," the butler said.

"Thank you," she said and squeezed the grey-faced, grey-haired man's grey hand.

"But the sooner you can get our . . . guest out of the house the better. She has been given a meal of best bacon, had a bath and been dressed in one of Lady Twistle's dresses and bonnets."

Nancy nodded.

There was a sudden rapping at the door like the volley of shots from Wellington's troop of soldiers.

"That could be just what we're waiting for," the butler said and turned to the door. He opened it.

Princess Victoria wandered around the room. She searched in the drawers of the dressing table. There were some corsets, stiff with whalebones, meant to hold in the body of an even larger lady than her.

Oh but it's a hard life being a whale. You are swimming around happily in the sea. Then, one day, someone stabs you with harpoons and drags you on to a ship. They skin you and gut you and what do they do with your bones? Wrap them round some large lady's body to squeeze her till she's thin. Me? I'd ban whale hunting, but I guess it will never happen.

There were bloomers and bustles, brooches and bracelets, powders and paints for her face. But no sign of the lady's name.

Then the princess found a small writing desk. Inside she found paper and a quill pen and a pot of black ink.

The room in which one was held prisoner has wallpaper with pale green and gold stripes. There is a dressing table in the French style: there is a writing table to match.

The hip bath one used has flower patterns on the side And one was given camomile soap with which to wash.

In a white-painted cupboard there are
clothes for a lady with a waist of fifty
inches which are held in with a corset to
make her forty inches. (One is far too small
to fit them oneself.)

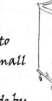

 Her black shoes are made by
hand and are large enough to put on a
lake and sail one's pet dogs. Enormous.

There are two brooches – cheap glass one should
say, three rings, a diamond and ruby
necklace, and a silver bracelet (too
large for one's own wrist).

The lady uses a lavender and rose scent, white face
powder and crushed red cheek powder.

With this description one is sure our
police forces will find the room where
one was held, put the villains on
trial and hang them for treason.

Princess Victoria

She folded the note, placed it in a purse that hung from her waist and sat on the chair by the writing table. She waited for the kidnappers to make their next move.

Constables Liddle and Larch stood in front of Inspector Beadle's desk in the basement of the police station. They were damp from a shower of drizzle on the outside and damp with sweat on the inside.

The gigantic inspector looked at them. "Yet again you have disgraced the Wildpool police force."

"Sorry, sir," Larch muttered.

"You let the kidnappers escape with a princess. They passed through the gate of the workhouse. Who was guarding that gate?"

"We were, sir," Larch muttered.

"We were, sir," Beadle mimicked. "The only way they could have got out of the workhouse was on the muck cart. The one that you didn't search."

"Well, sir," Liddle argued, "one piece of muck looks pretty much like the next piece of muck and we thought—"

"You *thought* . . . well that *is* new. Constables Liddle and Larch *thinking*!" the inspector roared till Liddle's moustache trembled in the blast.

"Get out there and find the muck cart . . . and arrest the drivers. Though I expect they will have escaped the town long before the Duke put up his road blocks."

They had. The two men went off to Darlham where they did a wonderful job of stealing night soil. In fact they did such a good job the Darlham Council paid them to work there. Two villains became two honest working men. It's a funny old world – smelly, but funny.

The two old constables tramped wearily up the stairs and on to the cobbled streets of Wildpool. People were gathering in huddles on street corners. "Who are they looking for?" the hat-seller asked.

"The Emperor of China, Mrs Potterwick has heard."

The hat-seller patted her dog on the head. "I bet my Alfie could sniff them out. He's trained, you know."

"What? To sniff out Emperors of China? How does he know what they smell like?"

"I own a china teapot," the hat-seller said proudly.

At 13 South Drive the butler opened the door. It wasn't Wellington's troops. It was Alice. She stood there in her scruffy-haired boy mask. She saw Nancy and waved the ransom note under her nose. "He signed," she said. "Get the princess."

"I wish I'd snatched Mrs Humble instead. The princess has been nothing but trouble."

"Don't worry, we can still make it work for the paupers of Wildpool. The princess's yacht is in the harbour. Let's get her back there, set Millie free from the workhouse, and we've done it."

Alice and Nancy ran upstairs and snatched a sack from a table at the top of the stairs. They tugged their masks firmly into place and unlocked the door. "We are setting you free."

"Has the Duke paid a fortune for our release?" Victoria asked.

"We don't want your money," Alice said. "Now we are going to take you back to the quayside."

"Is it far?" the princess asked carefully. "We are not used to walking far."

But Alice was too clever to walk into the trap. "You will never know how far it is. You'll be blindfolded so you can't trace the house."

"Our feet will know," Victoria cried. "Our poor little feet!"

"Then we'll take you in a wheelbarrow," Alice said. "Now, sit still while I place this sack over your head."

"Umm-mmm-mmmf mmmf?" came the royal voice.

Nancy raised the sack. "What?"

"We said . . . where did you get this stinking sack from?"

"From the sheep-head shop," Nancy said pulling it down.

"Umm-mmm-mmmf mmmf!!!"

You may think it's bad having your head stuffed into a stinking sack from the sheep-head shop. Baa! Just remember this: it was much worse for the sheep.

Chapter 13

BARROW AND BULLETS

"Please sir," Millie Mixley said to Mr Humble. "I have picked all the seeds from my cotton. Can I have *more* work?"

"We don't have any more cotton," Mr Humble snarled.

"No, sir, but perhaps I can help the women to pick oakum?" she said brightly.

"You *could* . . . but it's hard work. Makes your fingers bleed."

"I don't mind, sir. It's just so nice to live here I'll do anything to help!"

"The boy's sick," Humble muttered. "Must be

feeding him too much gruel." He unlocked the door into the women's work room. Thirty weary women took ropes and pulled them apart until they were left with a pile of loose strands. "There you go," he said. "You have half an hour then it's a quick spell in the exercise yard."

Mille nodded and said to herself, "Half an hour to take the pieces of rope and knot them into a rope ladder. A ladder long enough to reach the top of Wildpool Wonderful Workhouse's wall and down the other side."

The wheelbarrow rattled down the streets of Wildpool. The cargo under the sack wriggled and moaned, wobbled and whinged its way to the quayside. The troop of soldiers were gathering on the windswept deck of the yacht.

The wheelbarrow was tipped on to the cobbles and the two masked kidnappers ran up the hill towards the high street.

The Duke of Wellington paced up and down with a face as furious as a giraffe with neck-ache. "They can't have escaped the town by road or by sea. So where is she?"

"We are here," Princess Victoria snapped as she stamped up the gangplank and on to the deck.

"You are free, ma'am!" the Duke cried.

"No thanks to you," the pouting princess said sourly. "We have been kidnapped in a muck cart, held against our will, had a sheep-head sack wrapped over us and been transported in a wheelbarrow back here. Someone will have to be hanged. We cannot have these kidnapping criminals loose in our country!"

"And what did the kidnappers look like, ma'am?" the Duke asked.

"One looked rather like a cat . . . and the other was a very small boy with scruffy hair."

The wind blew wild down the valley and pushed the creeping constables back to Wildpool.

"My feet hurt," Liddle sighed.

"I'm hungry," Larch moaned.

"But we can't rest till we've arrested someone."

They passed the house with the sign, "Master Crook's Crime Academy" and stopped. "We could slip into the police station. Inspector Beadle will be in his office. He'd never know if we had a quick cup of tea

and a slice of bread and cheese," Liddle said.

Larch's mouth began to water and dribble like a baby's.

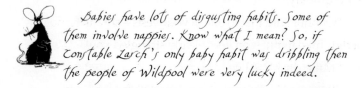

Babies have lots of disgusting habits. Some of them involve nappies. Know what I mean? So, if Constable Larch's only baby habit was dribbling then the people of Wildpool were very lucky indeed.

At that moment they saw a rare sight. Inspector Beadle stepped out of the doorway to the police station. He placed a large top hat on his large head and stepped into the street.

"We're supposed to be searching!" Liddle squeaked and dragged Larch back behind the gatepost of Master Crook's Crime Academy to hide till the danger was past.

Nancy and Alice panted up the steep hill, past Smiff's house. Smiff's mother, Mrs Smith, stood on the doorstep. "Ooooh! Hello there, Smiff," she said to Alice." "You should be wearing a hat – that's a nasty cold wind. We don't want you catching a fever, do we?"

"Hello, um . . . Mum, must dash," Alice said, backing away up the street.

"You've lost a bit of height, son," the woman said,

squinting at the retreating girl.

"Had a hot bath . . . I shrank in the wash," Alice said quickly.

"Ohhhh! I did that to one of your vests – shrank terrible it did. Tried to put it on you. Nearly strangled you!"

"Must dash!" Alice said.

"Been getting yourself a new cat?" the woman asked, pointing at Nancy.

"Yes . . . must go."

"Does it want a saucer of milk?"

"No. It only drinks blood. Bye!" Alice cried.

"Miaow!" Nancy said . . . and waved a paw.

The two girls sped up the street and turned into the High Street. The people on the corners were returning to their houses and work. "Looks like they found the Emperor of China then," the hat-seller said. "They're getting that yacht ready to sail." She stepped back into the hat shop, tugging her dog behind her on its squeaking wheels.

Alice slowed to a walk. "We've done it, Nancy!" she sighed as she stepped through the gates of the Crime Academy. "Safe at last!"

A long, white, bony hand rested on her shoulder. "I

arrest you in the name of the law!" Constable Liddle said. "You're the fella that was with the night soil men at the workhouse. Well, Wildpool's wonderful police force has triumphed again! I wouldn't be surprised if they don't hang you for this."

"What do we do with him?" Larch said, clamping handcuffs on Alice's thin wrists. "Inspector Beadle's just gone out."

"Let's take him to the Duke on the yacht. He'll know what to do."

"What about the cat?"

"Let it go," Liddle said.

"You mean let's not purr-sue it?" Larch joked.

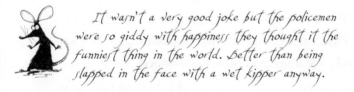

It wasn't a very good joke but the policemen were so giddy with happiness they thought it the funniest thing in the world. Better than being slapped in the face with a wet kipper anyway.

They dragged Alice into the High Street. Nancy raced into the school to report on the disaster that had struck.

In the workhouse Mr Humble was struggling to write his report.

WILDPOOL WORKHOUSE

DATE: FRIDAY 16TH MARCH 1837
REPORT: LOST PAUPER.
PAUPER NUMBER ONE IS MISSING. HE WAS WORKING IN THE OAKUM ROOM. AT
THE EXERCISE BREAK HE DID NOT RETURN. MAYBE HE WAS SO SKINNY HE
SLIPPED UNDER THE DOOR. THE WOMEN PAUPERS DID NOT TRY TO STOP HIM.
THEY WILL BE PUNISHED.

Mrs Humble looked over his shoulder. "Don't be stupid. If we report a lost pauper they'll stop paying for him."

"What do we do?"

"Find a uniform. Stuff it with oakum and sit it in his cell. We'll pretend he never escaped."

The yacht was almost ready to leave when Constables Liddle and Larch marched up to it and said, "We have the kidnapper! We have the kidnapper!"

The Duke came on to the deck followed by Princess Victoria. "Is this the villain?"

"You appear to have one of them," the princess said. "We wish to see him hanged."

"No time if we're going to catch the tide," the Duke said. He shouted orders and the soldiers ran back on deck. Then he spoke to Liddle and Larch. "Unfasten the prisoner's handcuffs. Cuff his hands behind him, around that lamp post, so he can't get away.

"Yes, sir," the policemen said and hurried to obey.

The Duke lined up the soldiers facing Alice. "It is our duty to execute this traitor. Line up. Aim for the heart."

"We don't wish to watch!" Victoria said and scurried below decks again.

"I think I'm going to be sick . . . again," Liddle groaned. He turned away.

"What have we done?" Larch gasped. "Let's get back and report to Inspector Beadle," he said and the old constables hurried off. At the bottom of Low Street they passed a group of people sprinting down the hill. The old men didn't even notice them. They just repeated, "What have we done?"

The soldiers stood in a row and raised their rifles. The Duke walked over to Alice. "Do you have a last request?"

184

"Yes," she said from behind her paper bag. "I'd like to die of old age if you don't mind."

"Request refused," the Duke said coldly. He stepped to the side. "Guards, take aim . . . and—!"

A small shape as quick as a rat's tail flew along the quayside. Millie Mixley threw herself between the firing squad and her friend Alice. "Remember Magna Carta!" she cried. "No free man shall be seized or imprisoned, except by the lawful judgment of his equals or by the law of the land."

The soldiers' muskets wavered a little. "The lad is right, sir," the sergeant said to the Duke.

"This is *treason*," the Duke explained. "He is guilty – you all heard the princess say so. Now. Take aim. . ."

Millie had not changed the Duke's iron mind. But she had put off the shooting for one precious minute. That minute was enough for the students and teachers of Master Crook's Crime Academy, who had listened to Nancy's tale, to hurry down to the quayside.

"Wait!" Samuel Dreep cried. He reached across and ripped off Alice's paper mask. "It's a girl! What sort of cowards shoot down a girl in cold blood."

The soldiers' rifles lowered again. "It's one thing shooting French soldiers at Waterloo," the sergeant said quietly. "For you, sir, we'd even shoot a traitor without a trial . . . but a little girl!"

The soldiers rested their rifles on the ground and turned away. The Duke's face glowed an angry pink in the cheeks. He drew a pistol from his belt. He aimed it at Alice's head. "I'm not scared of you," she snorted, looking him in the eye.

"Little girls don't plan kidnappings. Tell me who was behind this – we'll shoot them instead," the Duke said.

"Me!" Samuel Dreep said. "We planned to kidnap the workhouse keeper's wife – the princess was a mistake. But if you are going to shoot anyone shoot me!"

"Fine," the Duke said. "Sergeant, unfasten the girl. Put this man in her place."

The last person to arrive at the quay was the slowest. "And me!" Ruby Friday said. "You'll have to shoot me too. After all I am the real mastermind. The world's greatest kidnapper."

The colour ran from the Duke's face. "Ruby Friday?

After all these years?"

"Perhaps we'd better have a little word, before you shoot me," she said with a smile. In the watery light the Duke read the paper she held in front of him.

The Iron Duke's face became harder than iron.

BRITISH ARMY HEADQUARTERS, WATERLOO

17 June 1815

My Dear Bonaparte.

Just a little note to say I am looking forward to a jolly fine battle tomorrow. But I do hope you will lose! You see, British secret agents have kidnapped your dear wife Josephine. She is now my prisoner. She is comfortable but hidden somewhere that you will never find her.

Her guards have orders. If it looks like your French chaps are going to win the battle they will stuff your dear lady into a cannon and shoot her back to you. It could make a bit of a mess of your uniform with all those shiny medals.

This is frightfully unsporting, old chap, I know. But all is fair in love and war, as they say. Just make sure you <u>lose</u> the Battle at Waterloo tomorrow or we blow Jo. Send a reply with this messenger and we will spare the empress.

Best wishes and see you tomorrow,

Arthur Wellesley

Duke of Wellington and Baron Douro, Duke of Ciudad Rodrigo, Marquis of Torres Vedras, Count of Vimeiro.

By the time the Wildpool clock struck four o'clock the teachers and pupils of Master Crook's Crime Academy were walking up the hill and back to the school.

The yacht was sailing out of the river on the cold westerly breeze and the strong tide.

You will have forgotten what I said at the start. The mayor's wife of 1901 was quite right when she said "Queen Victoria never came to Wildpool". But the mayor's wife was quite wrong as well. See? Victoria came to Wildpool as a princess. She never came when she became queen. She refused! And she never allowed Wildpool to become a city. Now you know why!

On the quayside there were still the boatyards and barns and barges and ballast and bollards . . . but no bodies or bullets or blood.

The night began to close in on one of the strangest days in the strange history of Wildpool.

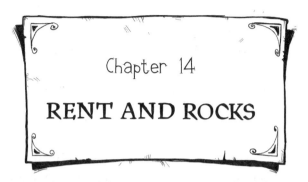

Chapter 14

RENT AND ROCKS

Saturday 17th March 1837

Lady Arabella Twistle sat in the dining room of 13 South Drive. The butler served soup silently.

"I promised to sack the Humbles and rebuild Garth Court," Mayor Oswald Twistle sighed.

"Nonsense," his wife snorted into her soup spoon. "They said they would tell the Duke that Princess Victoria was a prisoner in this house. So what? She is gone now. They can *never* prove that she was here. The Humbles stay. We save the money and *don't* build a new Garth Court with cheap rents to help the poor. Let the kidnappers go hang."

"If you say so, dear," Mayor Twistle sighed.

"I do."

The butler took the empty soup plates away. He hurried to the kitchen and scribbled a note.

N

I THINK YOU OUGHT TO KNOW. MAYOR TWISTLE WILL GO BACK ON HIS WORD. HE SAYS YOU CAN'T PROVE THE PRINCESS WAS HERE. SORRY. LOOKS LIKE THE WHOLE PLAN HAS FAILED.

B

He wrote "Nancy Turnip" on the front of an envelope. A maid was sent to deliver it to Master Crook's Crime Academy.

Monday 19th March 1837

On Monday morning the pupils met in the classroom of Master Crook's Crime Academy.

"Well, Ruby? What did you say to the Duke?"

Alice asked. "Mr Dreep would have been pushing up daisies by now if you hadn't done something."

Ruby smiled her apple-cheeked smile. "I told him he was a hero because he won the battle of Waterloo. But he wouldn't be a hero much longer if I told the world how he *cheated* . . . how *I* was the real hero that kidnapped Napoleon's wife! And I still have the note he wrote. Holy crumpets! He *had* to let you go."

"Princess Victoria wouldn't be pleased," Alice laughed.

"She wasn't," Mille Mixley said. "I saw her raging at the Duke as they sailed out of the harbour."

As I said, there were eight attempts to kill Victoria in her long life. Every one failed. Every time she demanded the assassin should be hanged. Every time she raged because they weren't! Vicious Victoria.

"So? What went wrong with our kidnap that almost got us shot?" Mr Dreep asked. "The best schools don't mind pupils making mistakes . . . but they *learn* from their mistakes. How did we end up with Alice and me in front of a firing squad?"

Smiff took a sheet of paper and wrote on it.

What went wrong?
Nancy snatched the wrong woman in
purple and white

Alice kept her disguise on too long

"But what have we got *right*?" Ruby Friday cried.
"Look on the bright side!"

WHAT WENT RIGHT?
MAYOR TWISTLE PROMISED TO SACK HUMBLE AND
REBUILD GARTH COURT

WE KIDNAPPED THE MOST IMPORTANT WOMAN IN THE
LAND ... AND ALMOST GOT AWAY WITH IT!

"And we won't make the same mistake next time.
Let's get on with planning the *next* kidnap," Samuel
Dreep said with an excited wave of rippling fingers.

"Who's the victim?"

Nancy took an envelope from her pocket and
passed it to the teacher. "Ah!" Dreep nodded. "I think
I have the answer. I will have a word with Master
Crook first."

Samuel Dreep took the letter and disappeared through a door that led into the basement at the Crime Academy. The basement room was almost dark, lit by a single candle. A door opened behind a curtain and a deep voice spoke. "Well, my friend Samuel. What do we have today?"

"A small problem, Master Crook."

In Wildpool police station, Constables Liddle and Larch stood in front of Inspector Beadle's desk.

He had two sheets of paper.

WILDPOOL POLICE FORCE

What went wrong?

Wildpool police allowed their VIP to be kidnapped under their very noses. They failed to find where she was held prisoner

"But what have we got *right*?" Liddle cried. "Look on the bright side!"

WILDPOOL POLICE FORCE

What went right?

The alert police spotted one kidnapper and delivered him to the Duke. Wildpool police managed to place one blind beggar in the workhouse

Inspector Beadle nodded. "As usual, gentlemen, Wildpool police have succeeded in keeping the town safe from the villains who roam its gutters. And you get to keep your jobs. . ."

"Thank you, sir!"

". . .for another month at least."

"Ah!"

Tuesday 20th March 1837

In the Crime Academy basement room the next day Lady Twistle sat and faced the curtain. A sheep-head shop sack was pulled off her head and left her with a red face and battered bonnet. "This is disgraceful. Someone will hang for this!"

She turned and looked at the kidnapper who had led her down the stairs. For this kidnap Alice had painted her paper mask with the face of Lady Twistle herself. "Urrrrgggggh!" Arabella Twistle cried. "What an ugly old woman!"

She was right!

"If anyone is to hang it will be you, Lady Twistle," the deep voice said from behind the curtain.

"Eh?"

"Princess Victoria was held prisoner in your house, your room. When the Duke of Wellington finds out you will be arrested."

Her ladyship's mean eyes looked suddenly as sly as a dog in a sausage shop. "Ah, but you can never prove that!" she cackled.

Alice unfolded a piece of paper and held it so Lady Twistle could read it. The note was written by Princess Victoria. It described the room where she had been held prisoner . . . Lady Twistle's room. The woman tried to look defiant but she only looked defeated.

"I slipped this out of the princess's purse before we dumped her out of the wheelbarrow," Alice explained.

Friday 30th March 1837

The families from Garth Court were given a day off by the new workhouse keeper, Ruby Friday. The well-fed and happy groups crossed the bridge and wandered down to the riverside. A fine new building was rising in the place where Garth Court had stood.

A sour-faced Mayor Twistle and his wife stood behind a table in the weak sunlight. Spring was struggling to come to the skies over Wildpool. But summer seemed to have arrived for the paupers. One by one families signed up to take new rooms when they were finished.

"How much?" Mr Jones (the organ grinder) asked.

"One shilling a week," the mayor said through his teeth as though the words hurt him.

"That's cheap!" Miss Jones (the street-singer) said.

"We can easily make it double . . . treble!" the little man said quickly.

Behind him a small figure stood. She had a face that looked very much like Lady Twistle's. She coughed. "The Princess Victoria note," she said.

Mayor Twistle took a deep breath. "One shilling . . .

no more," he sighed.

"I'll take it!" Miss Jones laughed.

"I thought you might," the mayor said.

The workhouse was almost empty. Only the blind beggar and two new inmates were there. The woman sweated over piles of ropes, unpicking them till her fingers bled to make oakum.

The man, in the men's yard, ached as he smashed large rocks into small stones and sweat ran down his forehead.

Ruby Friday brought the register up to date.

Date	Name	Class	Age	No
22 Mar 1837	Harper, Hengist	M	33	101
	Harper, Angela	W	39	102

The blind beggar was not working. As Hengist Harper slaved over the broken rocks the blind beggar

looked on. "I can't break rocks – I'm blind! I may hit someone over the head by mistake! Anyway, I have a visitor." The High Street hat-seller had taken an hour off to visit him with his dog.

"Are you happy here?" she asked.

"Happier since Miss Friday arrived," the beggar said. "And you?"

"Happier since I have your dog with the waggly tail for company!" she giggled.

"So," the beggar said. "Everybody's happy!"

Hengist Harper looked up. He looked as if he wanted to use that hammer on someone's head.

Which just goes to show . . . not everyone can have a happy ending.

LOOK OUT FOR MORE
MASTER CROOK'S CRIME ACADEMY
ADVENTURES

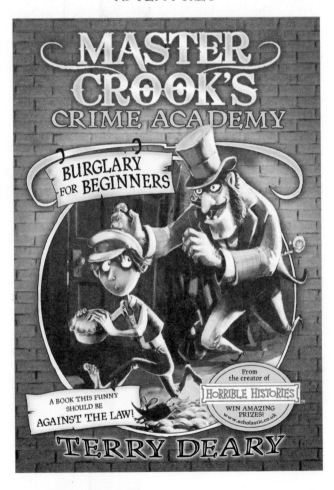

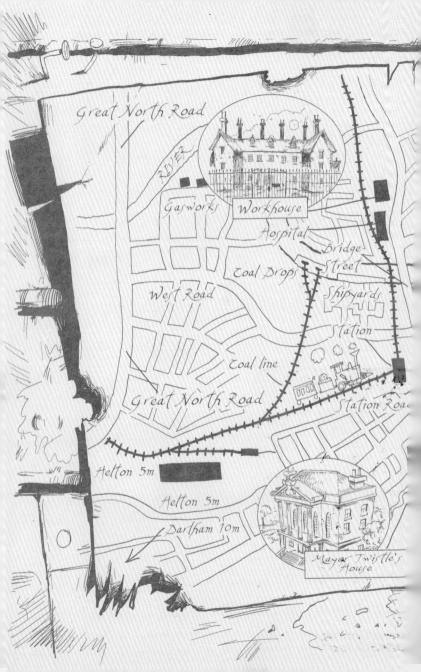